PARROT PIE FOR
BREAKFAST

PARROT PIE FOR BREAKFAST

AN ANTHOLOGY
OF WOMEN PIONEERS

Jane Robinson

OXFORD
UNIVERSITY PRESS

OXFORD

UNIVERSITY PRESS

Great Clarendon Street, Oxford OX2 6DP

Oxford University Press is a department of the University of Oxford.
It furthers the University's objective of excellence in research, scholarship,
and education by publishing worldwide in

Oxford New York

Athens Auckland Bangkok Bogotá Buenos Aires Calcutta
Cape Town Chennai Dar es Salaam Delhi Florence Hong Kong Istanbul
Karachi Kuala Lumpur Madrid Melbourne Mexico City Mumbai
Nairobi Paris São Paulo Singapore Taipei Tokyo Toronto Warsaw

with associated companies in Berlin Ibadan

Oxford is a registered trade mark of Oxford University Press
in the UK and in certain other countries

Published in the United States
by Oxford University Press Inc., New York

British Library Cataloguing in Publication Data

Data available

Library of Congress Cataloging in Publication Data

Parrot pie for breakfast: an anthology of women pioneers/selected
by Jane Robinson.
Includes bibliographical references (p.   ) and index.
1. Women pioneers—Great Britain—Colonies—History Sources.
2. Frontier and pioneer life—Great Britain—Colonies Sources.
3. Great Britain—Colonies—Social conditions Sources.   4. Great
Britain—Colonies—Social life and customs Sources.   I. Robinson,
Jane, 1959– .
HQ1593.P37   1999   305.4'0941—dc21   99–25636
ISBN 0–19–288020–9 (paperback)

3 5 7 9 10 8 6 4 2

Typeset in Ehrhardt by
Cambrian Typesetters, Frimley, Surrey
Printed on acid-free paper
in Hong Kong

To Caroline F. Schimmel

Acknowledgements

It is not the research that worries me about a book. It is not even the blank page that begins the weeks of writing. *This* bit is the real challenge. The responsibility of including all those who have helped produce this anthology is huge, and I am well aware that the whole thing has been a joint effort between us all.

I must thank the collector and authority on women in America Caroline Schimmel, to whom it is dedicated, first of all. No one could get anywhere on a project like this without her advice, which, together with unlimited access to her peerless library, was generously given right from the start. I am indebted to the trustees of the Alice Horsman Travelling Fund at Somerville College, Oxford, who kindly awarded me a research grant to visit Caroline's library near New York. Various other librarians and archivists have helped enormously, including those at the American Museum at Claverton Manor, Bath; the Battye Library, Perth (W. Australia); Birmingham University Library; the Bodleian at Oxford (particularly Rhodes House Library); the British Library; Ellis Island, New York; the Fawcett Library; the Maritime Archives and Library, Liverpool (particularly the archivist Gordon Read); the National Libraries of Australia and New Zealand; and New York Public Library.

For help in unearthing material I am grateful to Jan Bassett, A. C. E. Caldicott, Amy Cockett, Ronald Coghill, Anne Kahane, Mary Kempster, Angela Lind, C. Main-Braye, Helen Mogford, Jocelyn Murray, Janet Pearson, Valerie Ruddock, Margaret Sinclair, Mr and Mrs Tite, June Underwood, and May Williamson.

Finally, special personal thanks to Sheila Baird, Hattie Eastcott, Milbry Polk and the Schimmels for looking after me so well during my own very temporary settlement in the States; to my agent Fiona Batty and editor George Miller; to my cousin Shirley Bell (who inspired me through wild and wonderful tales of a Lincolnshire lass in Australia—she has come to rest there after years prospecting it in a camper van); to my mother Helen Robinson; to Richard and Edward for keeping my feet so comfortably on the ground; and last (and first) of all, to Bruce.

Contents

Introduction

One has to start somewhere. It is just a shame that I had to start with Mrs Roche and Mrs Humphries. Some of my more cynical friends were rather less than encouraging when the idea of this book was first mentioned, and assured me that the only women emigrants I was likely to find to include in it (once we had got the Walton family and *Little House on the Prairie* out of the way) would surely be those terrifyingly capable frontierswomen who went about spitting and saying 'yee-hah', their meeker pioneer sisters who bore babies and made potato cakes all day in squalid log cabins, or else the large-bosomed, lofty-nosed daughters of Empire who treated the whole world (or at least those large parts of it shaded satisfyingly pink on the globe) as their own slightly wayward parish.

'Rubbish: you are overgeneralizing,' I said. And, then, right at the beginning, I came across these two. Mrs Roche is an Englishwoman left all aflutter by the setting of yet another jewel in the British Imperial crown:

Annexation of the Transvaal! Where *is* the Transvaal? . . . Why, what do us want with another colony? Ain't the old hen done hatching yet? . . . Another chick! and why not? Moreover what would the poor mite do if this same good old foster-mother hen did not spread out her wings to give it warmth and shelter, to fend for it and to feed it? It has been in sore straits of late, little venturesome thing, and now gladly responds like a sensible bird to the welcome 'cluck! cluck!' . . .

HARRIET ROCHE, *On Trek in the Transvaal*, 1878

And here is the edifying Mrs Humphries:

It ought to be part of our patriotic feeling to endeavour to convey as agreeable an idea as possible of ourselves to those countries which we honour with our distinguished presence in our little trips.

MRS C. E. HUMPHRIES, *Manners for Women*, 1897

My heart began to sink. Although *I* might find such excess irresistible, a whole anthology of this sort of thing could get embarrassing. Next, I came across the story of Miss Moore in Alaska, whom you will find in the 'Danger and Desperation' chapter of the book: at first glance, it was distressingly easy to imagine her spitting in company.

Finally, in those first few days of preparation, someone sent me a photograph. It was Australian, dating from the end of the nineteenth century, and showed what looked like a woodpile with windows, with a couple at the door and three children standing on the scrubby ground outside. The squalid-pioneer variety, I thought—until I noticed that at one of the ill-assorted windows hung delicate, white net curtains. And the children were each dressed in spotless, ruffled pinafores and little button boots. There was a glow of real pride about this ramshackle scene, and I wanted to hear the voice of the woman at the door. I wanted to know why she was there, where she had come from, how she managed, and what she thought of her new life. The book was begun.

Once I started work in earnest on this story of homes from home, the gulf between Mistresses Roche and Humphries, Miss Moore, and this unknown Australian mother began to people itself with an astonishing variety of women. I had rather blithely thought I was reasonably familiar with the social history of British colonialism already, having read several settlers' accounts whilst researching previous books on women travellers. They were only *books*, though, and so only told the stories of those auspicious enough to have written or published them. The ordinary, small voice of a girl, writing laboriously (and well nigh illegibly) from the middle of some Ontarian nowhere to tell her sister in London how desperately she missed fish and chips, for example, or the bewildered terror of another, caught up in the Indian Mutiny of 1857: these were the characters most eloquent about what it was really like to be an emigrant woman.

I wonder what it was like to meet one. It would have been fascinating to be able to hear the response of native inhabitants to these strange, possessive settlers. We know a good deal by implication, of course. The massed and violent reactions of aboriginal peoples in the Antipodes, the Indian sepoys during the Great Mutiny, the North American Indians from the seventeenth to the nineteenth centuries—all these (instanced in the anthology) illuminate the relationship between these women and their new compatriots.

More obliquely, the very words of the women themselves, grotesquely ignorant and arrogant or plangently sympathetic as they might be, suggest how they must have been received by their neighbours. Contemporary written evidence, however, is hardly to be had, although much of what I *have* found is here.

As often as not, the most beguiling stories in the anthology were unearthed in diaries or letters; on scraps of cherished notepaper in family collections or anonymous-looking cardboard library boxes: some already (often obscurely) published; others not. I must admit that, on reading most of the stories they told—especially those included here in 'Spending the Day' and 'Matters Domestic'—it is hard to imagine when these women had the time to write. But then, I have heard more than one of them saying that if they had not had the luxury of talking unrestrainedly to a diary, or of listening to themselves for a few minutes each day (or each week, or once in a while), then they would have sunk. And the greatest pleasure of emigrant life for almost every woman I have come across was the receipt of mail from home. It was a lifeline, which could only be sustained by reciprocation.

All of which is not to say, of course, that I found printed books—books by emigrant women describing emigrant life—of little use. Even though they may give a more stylized view of the writer's experience, that view is no less valid. It is the public face of a very private adventure, and as interesting for what is left unsaid as what is said. I have drawn heavily on these accounts (most, long out of print) throughout the anthology.

This tension between public and private history became more evident to me as the book progressed. The public image of all these women is beset by generalities and caricature. Think of Mistresses Roche and Humphries, for example. It did not take long for me to realize, however, that, although they may have seemed somewhat larger than life, they were only certain women of their time. Mrs Roche's image of a broody Britannia reflected her own perception of duty: it was ladies like her who must themselves—for the good of the Empire—become mother hens, comforting, nourishing, and generally nest-building, however distant their roost. But, by no means did she speak for all her countrywomen. Some did not give a fig for patriotic duty—like Mrs Hall, marooned on the prairie in the 1880s:

Its vastness, dreariness, and loneliness are appalling . . . My advice to all emigrants is to leave their pride to the care of their families at home before they start. I would not live in such a place for worlds.

MRS CECIL HALL, *A Lady's Life on a Farm in Manitoba*, 1884

And the following is a client of the Female Middle Class Emigration Society (one of many such enterprising organizations, including the Self-Help Emigration Society and the United Englishwomen's Emigration Association). She is a teacher, writing home from Dunedin, New Zealand, in 1864:

Believe me, it is a hard struggle for a lady to succeed in this country . . . It is no use for a well-educated lady over 30 years of age to come out. I may do better in time, but I do not expect it for no person could work harder. It is a great mistake to fancy that an unprotected woman can make money in a Colony.

'MISS C.', from *New Horizons: a Hundred Years of Women's Migration*, 1963

So much for mother hens.

What about those emigrant spinsters who figure so largely in the statistics of colonial settlement? 'The life of the bush is a rough one,' wrote one Australian emigrant in 1852, 'but not without its charms. It would be perfectly fascinating were it not for the dearth of wives.' Another contemporary commentator conveniently lumped this wife fodder together as 'a super-abundance of females':

If the surplus female population with which we are overrun increases much more, we shall be eaten up with women. What used to be our better self will become our worst nine-tenths; a numerical majority which it will be vain to contend with and which will reduce our free and glorious constitution to that most degrading of all despotisms, a petticoat government . . . The daughters of England are too numerous and if their mother cannot otherwise get them off her hands, she must send them abroad into the world.

Punch, 1850

I should not think the powers that be were seriously worried about the perils of a 'petticoat government', but it did, at least, make some economic sense to ship these surplus females out, and turn what was becoming a liability into an asset. Those of them who fell into the distressed-gentlewoman or wholesome-hard-worker categories could be so useful in swelling the infrastructure of the Empire with pure-blooded stock of good Christian influence, after all. The rotten apples (prostitutes, convicts, or mere paupers) were quite simply better out of the country than in it.

Incidentally, one of the reasons there were so many spinsters about, especially during the nineteenth century, was simply the lack of eligible men at home. Any potential husbands were either desperately trying to gather together enough money for a family in an increasingly difficult job market in Britain, or else fighting and dying for their country—or, of course, out Empire-building themselves.

So, there is no doubt that there was a superabundance of females, but they were not just an Imperial commodity. They were individuals, whose sidelight on the social history of colonialism is all the more valuable for its obscurity. Few of the writers here had political or moral axes to grind: they were not important enough for that. Instead, they describe the domestic mechanics of settlement, the day-to-day details of what, for most of them, were strange and difficult circumstances; they describe feelings, impressions, and emotions in a world where too often survival was a starkly empirical affair. Theirs is the private history of emigration, if you like, pieced together with the mere particulars of life.

The wider the range, I hope, the clearer the picture: I have included over a hundred women in the anthology, spanning the age of Empire from the early seventeenth century to the early twentieth. Almost half of them are settlers in North America and Canada, a quarter in Africa, many in Australasia and India, and the rest scattered about the globe from Egypt to Jamaica, Sarawak to Samoa, and most points in between (not necessarily pink . . .). Just dipping into this anthology as I write its Introduction, for instance, I come up with Lady Harriot Dufferin, bogged down by the etiquette of being the Governor-General's wife in Ottawa; then, Elizabeth Justice, forced in 1734 to find work in Russia to pay off the debts occasioned by her former husband's refusal to pay a divorce settlement. Another 'wronged' woman—Fanny Stenhouse, a Mormon convert once the apple of her husband's eye and now, exiled in Utah, just one amongst many Mrs Stenhouses—follows Ellen Clacy, relishing the risky charms of gold-digging in Victoria; while the missionary Mrs Judson longs for someone to talk to— anyone—in the lonely Burmese village in which she lives.

Being rather fond of the exceptions supposed to prove rules, I have included amongst this collection of British women emigrants both non-British voices and those of more temporary settlers: the occasional American migrant, for example (although they have plenty of books to themselves), and one or two travellers merely staying abroad for a year or two. And even though I set the outbreak of the First World War as my chronological limit, there are a few voices harking back from more modern times. As a framework, I have used what little common experience my emigrant women shared: the chapters are arranged under headings like 'Taking Leave', 'The Voyage Out', 'First Impressions', 'Settling In', and so on. Thereafter, apart from brief introductions to each chapter and the odd link between extracts, they speak for themelves.

The separate voices of the women in this book are echoing still around the world, in the places their families now call home. And imagine all those emigrant women, the majority amongst the hundreds of thousands who left Britain between 1606 (when the first settlement was established in Virginia) and 1914, who did *not* write about their lives: this anthology is in remembrance, and celebration, of them all.

J. H. R.

Haddenham,
June 1998

ONE

TAKING LEAVE

Saturday, 4th. November, 1893! A new country has been added to the British Empire. Hip-hip-hurrah!
From *Experiences of Rhodesia's Pioneer Women*, 1938

*O*nly *a Jenny could have written that. Jenny was the name given to a character expressly designed, in a jaunty little pamphlet of 1869, to tempt away Britain's surplus females to the colonies. She was a paragon: feminine, strong, enterprising, hard-working, intellectual enough to satisfy (without surpassing) any potential husband's needs—and ignorant.*

There are Jennies abundant throughout the literature of emigration: women to whom the idea of venturing out into a pink-hazed Empire appealed on dutiful grounds, or romantic ones, perhaps for political or religious reasons or even in the pursuit of wholesome adventure. But most of them never actually left home: they just exhorted others. Or, if they did go, like those in the following few extracts, their idealism tended to evaporate in the unaccustomed and harsh light of practicality.

Of course idealism was not the only spur. Not all women emigrants were Jennies. Taking leave here are transported prostitutes; women forced from home to earn a living; those whose wifely obedience obliged them to go abroad; even one to whom the stench of British prejudice was so rank in the 1840s that she fled to America to escape.

Once it has been decided who is going, and why, and with what likely prospects, there are some words of advice offered in the way of preparation for the voyage out in this first chapter. Things like how to arrange one's packing cases, papers,

I

wardrobe, and—altogether more messy—one's emotions. Unless you're a Jenny, that is; for a Jenny's emotions come ready-organized. Like the rest of her.

Let every Johnny take his Jenny. Farmers' sons know farmers' daughters. Still, as a little rough work has to be done, even there, to ensure success, the Jenny that fights shy of the dairy, that sends the maid to gather the eggs, that holds her nose in her father's farm-yard, that can't bear the pigs, and dislikes the honest brown hand, had better not be chosen by the adventurous swain. I have one in my eye who is up with her mate at the lark's gay note, who milks the cows while he is with the horses or bullocks, greets him with smiles at breakfast, sends him off with a lunch to the fields while she carols at her labours at home, receives him at eve with a sunny face and a famous meal, and knows how to beguile the resting hour with intelligent talk.

W. TWEEDIE, Emigration! Where Shall I Go?, 1869

Is that all? The reality of an emigrant woman's role abroad was usually somewhat less simple. If she had a role at all.

Woman, I discover, is not indispensable to a man's comfort in Rhodesia. With the intelligent and adaptable native to minister to his wants, the bachelor can achieve a considerable degree of comfort of a rude kind, and is able to indulge to the full in all sorts of slack habits specially induced by the African climate. Shaving at long intervals, pyjamas all Sunday, smoking *ad. lib.* in bed, with breakfast at all hours—these are some of the indulgences which a wife may be expected to interfere with, and which must be balanced against the delights of matrimony.

The African bachelor is never driven into marriage by the monotony of having to do his own washing up. The more necessary is a sense of proportion for the new and reforming wife. The worst of it is that a sense of proportion which worked unfailingly in Kensington or Mayfair may be hopelessly at fault in mid-Africa. One needs a sort of graduated scale for every mile that takes one away from what is politely called 'civilization'. Perhaps a sense of humour is a good substitute, and this one certainly wants in ratio as one gets farther and farther from the ready-made world and deeper and deeper into the world where one must make everything for oneself—food, drink, amusements, comforts, all the things that seem to be laid on like the electric light at home.

ETHEL JOLLIE, *Some Humours of Housekeeping in Rhodesia*
[in *Blackwood's Magazine*], 1916

If Her Majesty's Government be really desirous of seeing a well-conducted community spring up in these Colonies, the social wants of the people must be considered. If the paternal Government wishes to entitle itself to that honoured appellation, it must look to the materials it may send as a nucleus for the formation of a good and great people. For all the clergy you can despatch, all the schoolmasters you can appoint, all the churches you can build, and all the books you can export, will never do much good without what a gentleman in [Australia] very appropriately called 'God's police'—good and virtuous women.

CAROLINE CHISHOLM, *Emigration and Transportation*, 1847

A man ought to consider, that women, and especially women with families, have been long bound to their homes; to their neighbourhood; to their small circles; most frequently much in the company of their mothers, sisters, and other relations; and that, to tear themselves from all these, and to be placed amongst strangers, and that, too, with the probability, and almost the certainty, of never seeing their circle of relations and friends again; and to begin their departure on the wide ocean, the dangers of which are proverbial, and perfectly terrific to female minds; for a woman to do all this, without the greatest reluctance, is too much for any reasonable and just man to expect; yet, if the *necessity* arise, it is still his duty towards his children, and even towards the wife herself, to persevere in the effecting of his object . . .

WILLIAM COBBETT, *The Emigrant's Guide*, 1829

3

And should one not be blessed with a Jenny:

All these things should be represented to a wife; her wailings should be heard with patience; even perverseness should be borne with as far as possible, if perverseness should, unhappily, possess her; but, after every possible effort has been made to reconcile her to the enterprise, go she must, or stay behind by herself.

Ibid.

As soon . . . as the resolution to emigrate has been fixed, let the females of the house make up their minds to take a cheerful and active part in the work of preparation. Let them at once cast aside all vain opposition and selfish regrets, and hopefully look to their future country as to a land of promise, soberly and quietly turning their attention to making the necessary arrangements for the important change that is before them.

CATHERINE TRAILL, *The Female Emigrants' Guide*, 1854

The lady who proposes to go to Nigeria should possess those two useful things, a stout heart and a strong constitution: the first to enable her to overcome objections that will be raised on all sides to her going at all, and the second to weather the climate and the hardships she will encounter when she gets there. She will find it greatly to her advantage if she is also one of those contrary and high-spirited people who thrive on opposition, the kind of person who derives an unholy joy from doing that which is forbidden—no matter what it may be—who would rather climb over a wall and steal apples than walk soberly into a shop and buy them. In short, if she has an enterprising and ardent disposition and a soul athirst for adventure, she cannot choose a better outlet for her activities than a journey into Nigeria . . .

MRS HORACE TREMLETT, *With the Tin Gods*, 1915

Few white men are in Africa for pleasure, fewer still for profit, but all are here for service of one degree or another; hence the man in Africa finds his life more or less definitely marked out for him by the powers that be in the mother country. He may be engaged in scientific research, in the study and government of the millions of native inhabitants, or he may lend himself to some infant commercial enterprise; but, whatever his calling, his work is well defined, and brings recognisable results. The woman, on the other hand, is the 'little bit of fluff,' the negligible quantity which gives an added note of colour to the surroundings, and chiefly because of her rarity she receives a higher valuation than at home.

Upon her falls the delicate task of keeping alive the perception of true womanhood in all men who have left their women-folk and home ties for long periods of inhibition in uncivilised countries. She must be cheery in sickness and in health; for her own salvation she must feel and express an intelligent whole-hearted interest in the work of these men, whatever its degree of importance; her hospitality must exceed the bounds of mere studied politeness, for the Africanised European is far quicker to perceive a lukewarm perfunctory welcome than is his brother in England.

'To be pleased with everything and please everyone in the place' should be an eleventh commandment in the outposts of the Empire.

ANN DUNDAS, *Beneath African Glaciers*, 1924

To those of my own sex who desire to emigrate to Australia, I say do so by all means, if you can go under suitable protection, possess good health, are not fastidious or 'fine ladylike,' can milk cows, churn butter, cook a good damper, and mix a pudding. The worst risk you run is that of getting married, and finding yourself treated with twenty times the respect and consideration you may meet with in England. Here (as far as number goes) women beat the 'lords of creation;' in Australia it is the reverse, and there we may be pretty sure of having our own way.

ELLEN CLACY, *A Lady's Visit to the Gold Diggings*, 1853

Ellen Clacy ran the risk and found herself a husband in Australia. Their honeymoon was a voyage straight back home to England. For her, emigration—however temporary—was a happy choice, while for others it was no choice at all.

I never did, and God grant I never may again, witness so much misery as I was forced to be a spectator of here: Among the outcasts were seven of our own countrywomen, decrepid with disease, and so disguised with filth and dirt, that I should never have supposed they were born white; add to this, almost naked from head to foot; in short, their appearance was such as I think would extort compassion from the most callous heart; but I declare they seemed insensible to shame, or the wretchedness of their situation themselves . . .

I always supposed these people had been transported as convicts, but some conversation I lately had with one of the women, has partly undeceived me. She said, the women were mostly of that description of persons who walk the streets of London, and support themselves by the earnings of prostitution; that men were employed to collect and conduct them to Wapping, where they were intoxicated with liquor, then inveigled on board of ship . . . 'Thus,' in her own words, 'to the disgrace of my mother-country, upwards of one hundred unfortunate women were seduced from England to practise their iniquities more brutishly in this horrid country.'

A. M. FALCONBRIDGE, *Two Voyages to Sierra Leone*, 1794

The Occasion of my going into *Russia* was owing to my Husband, who was to have pay'd me an Annuity of Twenty Five Pounds a Year; Which he omitting to pay for Five Years, and a Quarter; I then, contrary to my own Inclination, was oblig'd by my Sufferings for want of that Money, to go to Law; and I did obtain a Verdict in my Favour: At which he was so much displeas'd, that he declar'd, He would proceed in Chancery against me, if I did not pay the Law-Charges that had been expended; and, rather than have a Suit in Chancery, I chose to pay the Expences. But this unhappy

Circumstance render'd me incapable of paying my just Debts: However, to overcome that Difficulty, I propos'd to have my Annuity apply'd for the Payment of them, as it became due, which he agreed to; he promising for the future to pay it punctually; and then I resolv'd to go abroad to acquire a Support 'till my Creditors were satisfied.

Upon enquiring amongst my Friends for a Family that wanted a Governess, I soon heard of a Gentlewoman that was going into *Russia*, who had Occasion for such a Person as I was for a LADY of her Acquaintance at Petersburgh.

ELIZABETH JUSTICE, *A Voyage to Russia*, 1739

I have seen my various friends bankrupt,—myself have known the anguish of hunger and want;—and what indeed is worse, I have been long a sufferer from the stupid and cruel prejudices of my country, which exclude all females who labour either with their fingers or with their heads, *for remuneration*, from the rank and privileges of gentlewomen. By reason of these purse-proud and vulgar prejudices, I was condemned by a Father's pride, and a Mother's tenderness, to abstain from every effort which might have contributed to their comfort or my own, and from gratifying my own feelings of independence by being actively useful. A woman in England, in consequence of the highly artificial state of our society, who rises superior to the frowns of fortune, *in fact she who works*, is looked upon as degraded, as separated for ever from the class in which she was born; this false pride, and this abject fear of the loss of *caste*, warp and destroy the energies of many of my countrywomen. Poverty, whether inherited or accidental, is no reproach in America—personal exertion, mental or physical labour, is regarded with respect and honour whether in a man or in a woman. Success is rewarded with congratulation, and disappointment is alleviated by sympathy, and by the aid which each is ready to extend to his neighbour.

SARAH MYTTON MAURY, *An Englishwoman in America*, 1848

If you are possessed of rank and money, stay in England; no where are these advantages so available. If you have neither . . . get away from it as fast as possible.

Ibid.

THE CHOICE OF OCCUPATION OFFERED

Canada:—Organist. Teacher of music. Housekeeper in a General Hospital. Nurse in charge of operating theatre. Employee of a Shipping Company. Research worker in a University. Secretary to Training School for Nurses. Head of social service work in connection with a Hospital. Stenographers in a large hotel and in a business office. Manager and owner of a tea shop in the Maritime Provinces. Proprietress of shop and of lending library. Port worker. Woman officer of Land Settlement Department. Head accountant to stockbroker.

Australia:—Companion to lady poultry keeper and dog breeder. House Mistress in Girls School. Secretarial position in a Government Department and in a business house. Teaching post under the Education Department. Governesses in private families. Employee in a hairdressing establishment. District nurse. Music teacher in a 'station' home. Assistant in a private café. Games Mistress in a private School. Lady Help in Guest House. Motor driver and Companion Help. Hotel Manageress. Welfare worker, School Matron. Milliner. Hospital Nurses, several specially trained for mental cases.

New Zealand:—Hospital trained nurses. Matron at Nurses' Home. Chauffeuse Lady Help on Sheep Station. Welfare Worker. Art Needleworker. Private Governesses. Assistant in hairdressing establishment. Teachers of Music, Arts and Crafts, Elocution, Physical Culture and Domestic Science, and Games Mistresses.

SOCIETY FOR THE OVERSEA SETTLEMENT OF BRITISH WOMEN, *How It Helps*, 1931

The possibilities appear almost endless. A stalwart spirit and a breezy sense of enterprise (we are back in the realm of Jennies here) will see you to the ends of the earth. Those, and the right wardrobe.

Linen skirts of any colour that is not too delicate are invaluable; half a dozen of them, one or two holland, and a couple of simple muslins or cool cottons, should carry you triumphantly through your time. The woman endowed with clever fingers can, of course, add to her stock, armed with good paper patterns, lengths of unmade material, and, if she is lucky, a sewing-machine, and she will probably be very glad of the occupation for her spare time. Shirts and blouses of thin flannel, washing silk and muslin can be brought in any number that space allows—the more the better, but the local laundry cannot goffer frills and almost always tears lace! Cambric and muslin blouses of the 'shirt' order are the most useful kind, as silk rots almost at once. For this reason let your smarter blouses be of *crêpe de chine* rather than silk. Evening gowns you will scarcely want; one, or at most two simple dinner frocks, and a tea-gown to wear for dinner at home, will be ample . . .

I think perfect comfort and happiness can be found in fine cambric or nainsook combinations, or spun-silk vests and cambric knickers. I rather doubt the desirability of washing-silk under-garments, chiefly because the art of laundry work is in its infancy, and the silk shirts that I have had washed have returned distinctly hard and harsh. But the main point, in a climate like this, is to have enough of whatever you decide to wear; you will probably change everything two or three times a day . . .

At least six pairs of corsets are necessary, the coolest kind obtainable, certainly, but I can assure you that to leave off wearing them at any time for the sake of coolness is a huge mistake: there is nothing so fatiguing as to lose one's ordinary support even with a view to being 'comfy.' *Always* wear corsets, even for *tête-à-tête* home dinner on the warmest evenings; there is something about their absence almost as demoralizing as hair in curling-pins! . . .

If it will not quite break your heart, be advised and brush back your fringe, if you have one; it is quite impossible to keep it in curl or tidy, and the peace and comfort you will get from the absence of clammy dank wisps of short hair will amply repay you for what you may think an unbecoming change. May I also whisper that no one should allow her friends at home to persuade her to invest in an 'artistic and invisible' 'transformation'; they are all too visible, and, for this country, are simply waste of money.

CONSTANCE LARYMORE, *A Resident's Wife in Nigeria*, 1908

For the wife [bound for 'the diggings']: Three cotton dresses, one pair stays, four petticoats, sixteen chemises, two flannel petticoats, twelve pairs cotton stockings, four pairs black worsted ditto, six night dresses and caps, six pocket handkerchiefs, four handkerchiefs for the neck, six caps, two bonnets, cloak and shawl, one pair boots, two pair shoes, and eight towels . . . The family will also require a mattress and bolster, one pair blankets, one coverlet, six pairs cotton sheets, two or three tablecloths, six pounds yellow soap, three pounds marine soap, metal wash-hand basin, knives and forks, one quart tin hook-pot, one coffee pot, comb and brush, besides a supply of string, sewing materials, tape, buttons, &c . . .

[I]t will always be desirable that the wife makes as many of her clothes as possible on board ship, as the occupation serves to pass many an otherwise idle, heavy hour . . .

Bulky furniture would be a costly incumbrance to anyone proceeding beyond the immediate neighbourhood of the shore. A portable iron bedstead, however, is worth taking. (And a tent.)

AN AUSTRALIAN JOURNALIST, *The Emigrant in Australia*, 1852

Tents.—All letters from the colony speak of these being an indispensable article of an emigrant's outfit.

Boxes must be made small, that a man may be able to carry them; but a *barrel* is a better packing-case, as then a man may roll it. Use it afterwards as a shelter at night; or turn it, if clever enough, into an easy chair.

Testimonials.—It is found of great service, as to the position of emigrants in the colony, to take out with them not only their registers of birth and marriage-certificates, but testimonials of character from their spiritual pastors, magistrates, corporation-officers, physicians, gentry, or known respectable persons in business.

Extras.—Those who have money to spare may take with them a few pounds of patent flour, a pound of arrow-root, some rice, tea, and sugar, and a jar of pickles. Those who have children should take preserved broths and milk.

CAROLINE CHISHOLM in *The Emigrant's Guide to Australia*, 1854

Choose a ship that is well ventilated—that is to say, go in a ship which has one sleeping deck for passengers rather than two; be careful that you can not only walk upright on this deck, but that it is at least seven feet from the deck above . . . with a proper current of air below. See that the ship has high bulwarks (wooden walls), at least six feet high, so as to prevent passengers from being drenched every time they come on deck. If you have a family choose a ship, if possible, which has separate water closets for males and females . . . [and] take with you some chloride of lime got from a chemist, and throw a little into the closet now and then, to stop bad smells.

The weak among my readers—and I would add the very poor but they cannot afford to choose—should be careful, if possible, to select a ship in which they are not required to cook for themselves. To the richer passengers who can bribe the cooks with half a crown now and then, to pretty women who can coax them with their smiles, or to strong men who can elbow their way with their broad shoulders, such advice is not necessary, as they can have access to the crowded cookhouse any time, and any number of times daily; but the others often have to wait for hours in the wet, or even all day, to cook a single meal . . .

VERE FOSTER, *Work and Wages; or, the Penny Emigrant's Guide*, 1855

Understandably, as the voyage approached, most women found it difficult to maintain that unwavering optimism that might (if they were lucky) have fuelled their preparations. Taking leave is, after all, the first irrevocable step in the adventure of emigration.

To Mrs Morley, Doncaster

Bawtry, March 30, 1825

Dear Madam,

It devolves upon me to give your daughter (whether I ought to call her Miss Margaret Morley, or Mrs Clough, I know not) some directions how to manage her health during the anticipated voyage to Ceylon. The difficulty of this duty is much lightened by knowing that Mr Clough is himself accustomed to the usual precautions required whilst at sea, and also habituated to the climate of the place whither they are bound.

Your daughter must calculate on sea-sickness; but its effects are not likely to be injurious to my patient's constitution; therefore, I have only to say, that if any thing be used in the shape of medicine at the commencement of the voyage, I think that soda-water will be the most agreeable and most appropriate medicine . . . If the skin assume a dry feverish feel, arising from the state of the atmosphere, Mrs C. will, I think, find this corrected by wearing a wash-leather vest over the linen. The use of a wash-leather waistcoat will also be a very great protection from the *unhealthy breezes*, and the oppressive state of atmosphere, which often occur on low swampy shores, and in situations where there is an excess of umbrageous vegetables, and consequently a stagnant air resting on decomposing vegetable matter. While on the subject of occasional clothing, I must recommend the head to be carefully protected by a light hat or bonnet, with a *double* pasteboard crown, so managed that a vacancy be left between the two sheets of pasteboard . . .

As to diet: let it be plain, but with more seasoning than when at Doncaster . . .

I offer no congratulations to you and Mr M. I write no complimentary wishes to Mr and Mrs Clough; but hope God, whom we serve, will deliver, and save [them] to the uttermost; and we shall meet in his kingdom.

MARGARET CLOUGH, *Extracts from the Journal*, 1829

TWO

THE VOYAGE OUT

Yesterday passed very much like the day before.
Miss J. Harcourt, *Diary on board the 'Great Victoria'*, 1864

It was so **boring**. *That is the overriding memory of one group of emigrant diarists of the voyage out from Britain. Weeks, months, sometimes more than half a year, in the same small space with the same small people and the same small amusements day after day. This group only includes those who could afford the luxury of tedium, however. They were emigrant ladies, rather than women, who were used to better things, and whose principal discomforts on board ship involved the general lack of high-calibre company.*

There were more palpable vexations, of course, the most dangerous of which were confined to the steerage compartments where as many bodies were packed into as small a space as possible. Apart from the squalor and sickness bound to arise from the conditions (resulting, in late eighteenth-century transport ships, in the habitual loss of at least half the human cargo), there was the treatment of the women by the crew to be considered. The (American) captain's manners were appalling, reports an English lady, Mrs Felton, on her voyage to New York in 1838. 'He was morose and remarkably ignorant—was perpetually smoking cigars, and, like his countrymen, eternally spitting'. But convicted criminal Mary Long did not mind the captain of her vessel too much at all. At least he shared his bed with her. So did some of the sailors. And the Catholic priest. In fact, one of those assorted gentlemen was the father of the child she realized she was carrying as the voyage progressed.

Several of the extracts to come prove that there were at least one or two (other) diversions available at sea. Cockroach counting was a good one, and wondering what might be served up for the next meal. In fact, the contemplation and consumption of food was of overwhelming interest to all passengers— especially as the weeks wore on—just as they are to prisoners everywhere. Any break in the usual routine was welcomed: the captain rather thrillingly smoking out the inhabitants of the steerage decks from time to time, for example, or the occasional washday or shipwreck. They all helped to pass the time until landfall.

For most emigrants, journey's end did not coincide with the ship reaching its final port: there was more travelling to be done, perhaps even a continent to cross, before any new home from home could be considered. Some said it was faith in the future that kept them going, but, for Miss Harcourt, it looks more like mere hope:

Last night the picture around us was most beautiful. The sky was almost cloudless, and the moon was full. There was a gentle breeze out, just enough to ripple the waves. The sea was of a deep, dark blue, except in one light, silvery track of moonlight, looking like a shining pathway to some happier land.

MISS J. HARCOURT, *Diary on board the 'Great Victoria'*, 1864

But, was she looking from the bow of the ship, I wonder, or its stern?

To more practical matters, now, and the recommended 'Regulations on Ship-Board' of the philanthropic Mrs Chisholm.

The following regulations were so successful in their intended object, as to comfort, health, happiness, and independence on shipboard, that we give them insertion for the guidance of those purposing a residence of three or four months in a floating iron or wood house.

Family Groups.—Each body of emigrants is divided into groups containing twelve adults, who can take their meals together during the passage. The object of this arrangement is, that friends and relatives may unite and aid each other in their common emigration . . . A list of the associated groups embarked, with their names and ages, the place from which they emigrated, their destination and subsequent settlement, the amount of loan advanced, repayment made, the sums still due and by whom, will be published as often as the committee may deem proper.

Protection to Orphan Girls and Friendless Families.—The friendless young women are grouped with and introduced to families (at the group-meetings held at Mrs Chisholm's residence, on Mondays, at seven o'clock in the evening, previous to embarking), and placed under their special guardianship. Arrangements are also made to insure mutual responsibility for good conduct during the passage . . .

Cabins.—Inclosed cabins are furnished to each family, of a size according to the number of individuals. Children above fourteen years of age are provided with compartments for sleeping separate from those of their parents. One inclosed cabin is allotted to seven single females, also an inclosed cabin for seven single men, in parts of the vessel appropriated by classification for those berths. The arrangement of the cabins is such as to provide for perfect order, decorum, and morality.

CAROLINE CHISHOLM in *The Emigrant's Guide to Australia*,
1854

Order, decorum, and morality were, of course, the ideal . . .

I saw a poor emigrant who had been too late for the ship engage a boat to bring her alongside; it was a very little distance; the men demanded three shillings for carrying herself and her sack of potatoes; she, poor soul, possessed but a few halfpence, which she offered—they were rejected with a loud laugh, and the men rowed away with the potatoes.

SARAH MYTTON MAURY, *An Englishwoman in America*, 1848

Of the single girls we had more than sixty on board our ship, and one fortnight's acquaintance with them had sufficed to show us that they were a most unpromising set; and moreover, our early impression that several of them had made acquaintance with the inside of a jail was not at all effaced by the experience and events of the voyage. One of them, whose hair when she came on board was cropped suspiciously short, accounted for it by saying that her sister-in-law used to pull it out when they had a quarrel; but she was not the only one who might have been supposed to have been under the hands of the prison barber, for several others were in a similar predicament as to the paucity, or rather brevity, of their locks.

There were perpetual complaints throughout the voyage, caused by the petty thefts committed upon one another by these damsels, such as purloining the steel from each other's crinolines, appropriating articles of clothing, little brooches, and such-like; but the favourite objects of cupidity were the photographs of other people's sweethearts, the abstraction of which was an act of aggression which seemed to demand the taking of some especial precautions for the general security, and accordingly the girls came one morning in a body to the captain, bringing with them a pile of likenesses, of which they solemnly requested him to take charge until the ship should reach Fremantle.

MRS EDWARD MILLETT, *An Australian Parsonage*, 1872

Revd Philip Connolly, catholic Priest, being duly sworn, states, I took my passage on board the Ship 'Janus' . . . about three weeks after I had been on board, I had reason to suspect some improper intercourse was going on between the female Convicts and the Sailors; my reasons for so doing were in consequence of some Conversation between the Surgeon and Captn.; the intercourse appeared to me to be general; I have reason to believe there were two or three Women often, indeed Constantly, in the Captain's Cabin; Lydia Elsden was one, Mary Long also was one; she endeavoured to get in of a night; they were in the sleeping Births and did not appear in the day; they were in the principal part of the day and principal part of the night. I felt it my Duty to have some conversation with the Captain in the course of a Month after we sailed. I did so frequently nearly the whole Voyage; there was a time I ceased to do it, Convinced it was useless; these things were frequently talked over publicly in the Cabin. Captain Mowat seemed by his words to wish to prevent it, but not by his Actions. I have reason to believe as to the Sailors, each took their partner from the Prison-room . . . I believe Prostitution was carried on during the Voyage to a most Shameful extent.

Mary Long, being duly Sworn, states, I was one of the female Convicts that came out in the Ship 'Janus' . . . When I have not been Confined in the Prison during the night, I have passed my time in the Captain's Cabin. I believe I am at this time in a pregnant Condition . . . When I was in the Captain's Cabin, it was Commonly known. When I went, I went publicly down night or day. I washed and mended for Captain Mowat. I constantly had occasion to go down for those purposes. Mary Hoare, Isabella Irvin used to wash for the Priests: Ellen Molloy cooked for them; they had frequent occasion to go into the Priests' Cabin . . .

HISTORICAL RECORDS OF AUSTRALIA, *Proceedings of the Bench . . . into Prostitution*, 1820

Among the few women on board was a petite young Englishwoman who had her innings each day by telling us what they did 'at home.' Her husband, to whom she alluded affectionately at all times as 'Jim dear,' was a fine specimen of the British type who belong to the remittance class.

'She felt vexed, in fact, she was a trifle angry, you know.' She sat up all night that she might be at the head of the procession and secure the very best berth to be had on the vessel, and spent the remainder of the day in boasting to her less fortunate fellow passengers. Her stateroom, which was the largest on the ship, 'you know,' had double berths, 'you know,' and the door opened into the social hall, 'you know,' and the window opened from the inside so 'Jim dear' could sit so comfortably by himself in his own stateroom and amuse himself, 'you know, watching the seals play hooky.' And

the stationary bowl was quite large enough, 'you know,' to afford a
b-a-u-t-h, 'you know.' Their tickets being first-class entitled them
to a seat at the captain's table, 'you know.' She was so glad she had
staid up all night and secured such excellent accommodations. She
felt so sorry, 'you know,' for others less fortunate. As for herself she
could ensure hardships rather gracefully, 'you know.'

LUELLA DAY, *The Tragedy of the Klondike*, 1906

The captain and his lady were, in point of disposition, the most
unlovely specimen of Americans I ever met with, either before or
since, and were, every way, calculated to give us a most
unfavourable opinion of the state of society in their country. Ever
since his first voyage to Europe, the captain had formed an
unfavourable opinion of the English, from two circumstances, that
none, but a person of his own cast of mind, would adduce as
distinguishing marks of the English character. I remember, one of
these grievances was, that some on the quay at Liverpool, had
applied to him the unpalatable term of 'transported Yankee,'
garnished with some accompaniments, by no means complimentary. For this, and something else equally important, he seemed to
consider himself justifiable in insulting every Englishman, and lost
no opportunity of stretching this assumed prerogative, when
conveniently practicable, to the very bounds of despotism.

He was morose and remarkably ignorant—was perpetually
smoking cigars, and, like his countrymen, eternally spitting; but a
very moderate drinker. Out of his profession he was nobody, but
we had good reason to believe, his nautical talents were of the high-
est order.

MRS FELTON, *Life in America*, 1838

There are some very nice Irish people on board and we generally are
together in a group on deck, chatting, sewing, reading, knitting, and
enjoying ourselves. Young Walker and his half-brother T. Sloane are
great friends with us, and there is a Miss Pedlow from Lurgan who

is very civil and obliging. I am not fretting as I expected. I hope to go home again sometime and see all the old familiar faces once more. Every night I am with them in my dreams . . . Our friends on board as a general rule are either Irish or Scotch. We don't mix much with the English. I am thoroughly sick of [them].

MRS FLEMMING in Patrick O'Farrell's *Letters from Irish Australia*, 1984

The heat of the cabins is not to be described; ours is suffocating. We have two stern windows, but they are of little use, as, the wind being constantly ahead of us, we can get no [fresh air]; and where there ought to be a side-port[hole] is a large looking glass, which only reflects one's dirt and discomfort. But I could endure all this, were it not for the swarm of cockroaches that infest us; they almost drive me out of my senses. The other day sixty were killed in our own cabin, and we might have killed as many more; they are very large, about two inches and a half long, and run about my pillows and sheets in the most disgusting manner. In order to guard myself against them, I am obliged to sleep with a great muslin veil over my face, which adds not a little to the heat and suffocation.

Rats are also very numerous. One night Mr Welby Jackson, one of the passengers, was asleep on the cuddy table, and was woken up by a huge monster running down one of the punka ropes into his shirt, and it was a long time before he could dispossess himself of his unwelcome visitor. The captain keeps a very good table, and has an excellent cook.

MRS GEORGE DARBY GRIFFITH, *A Journey Across the Desert*, 1845

Perhaps, given the right company, the voyage out could be a pleasant affair.

Be sure and tell my aunt that it is very charming to hear the cock crowing in the morning. The vessel was going very smoothly last night. The captain asked me if he would get a dozen of these sailors to run backwards and forwards to rock me to sleep.

ANNE ISABELLA SMITH, *Diary on board the 'Finland'*, 1848

I can always see everything that is going on outside from my berth. There are venetians which we let half down, & whenever anyone passes, Rachel & Miss Maunder call upon me to report who it is. We never can sleep for a long time after we go to bed so it is rather an amusement. We keep up a great noise in our cabin sometimes at night, or rather Rachel & Miss Maunder do, singing duets. The stewardess who sleeps next makes ineffectual double knocks on the wall—but we only knock back to tell her to go to sleep. We also keep up a sort of light skirmishing sometimes & pelt each other with missiles of various kinds in the shape of shoes, boots, pillows etc., lying comfortably in our berths all the time. I consider my position the most advantageous from its elevation, for bombarding. The aborigines are rather a drawback to repose & comfort. Rachel and I both get them occasionally, but not as often as I expected.

ANNIE HENNING, *The Sea Journals of Annie and Amy Henning*, ed. Joan Thomas, 1984

on board *Scottish Hero* off Cape of Good Hope
14th December 1883

My dear Mother,

We are now about half-way on our journey, and I hope during the other half to have written a good long letter. It seems nothing to look back on the past six weeks, although to you it must be like a year.

Well, one day was pretty much the same as another until a washing day was started. The carpenter had made a couple dozen tubs out of meat and flour casks, and as the weather was getting warmer (it was never colder than when we left Gravesend) this great washday commenced on a Monday. Groups of women were seen, some standing, and some kneeling on deck. Then comes the question of hanging out. We had to put up our own line, and when that was up we didn't like hanging up the linen—until a Portsmouth woman says 'Here goes,' and her chemise and drawers went off in full sail, catching all the wind. How we did laugh to be sure. The Captain and doctor fairly choked—they watched us from the poop. Mine were hanging up just over the butcher's table, and when the purser went to serve out the meat, my drawers kept flapping in his face, and he said 'By Jove, I wish this woman's somewhere else'. I wasn't far off on my camp stool, and could not keep from laughing.

The next day was another excitement. The boxes were taken up—every box was brought up on deck, and then we had about three hours to look out what clothes were wanted for the Tropics. It would have made a capital picture if anyone could have sketched it.

ANNA COOK, *Letters*, 1883–4

We are all put in good humour by passing four vessels bound in the same direction. We distanced them so quickly we had barely time to exchange signals. One of them was the *Early Morning* going to Port Natal. It came very close to us. There were three ladies on board and we waved our handkerchiefs to each other . . .

One of the pigs has taken the staggers, poor animal! They bled it, gave it sulphur, and cropped its ears, but it was of no avail. It died shortly afterwards and was pitched overboard . . .

The Captain is always planning something kind. He takes a great deal of trouble of setting us comfortably with arm chairs, footstools, etc. Then when he thinks we will do in that respect, the steward will appear laden with apples, iced water seasoned with limes, or lemons, sponge cake, sandwiches or some other dainty.

JESSIE SCOTT BROWN, *Jessie's Sea Diary 1861–2*,
ed. M. Fountain and M. Spathaky, 1994

For lack of other, fresher, topics of conversation, food and health were unfailingly popular.

[July 2nd, 1840] I shall note down a weeks bill of fare as we have a *diet* for every day. Breakfast ham & egg potatoes, tea & coffee biscuit & treacle wch we always have morn^g & even^g Dinner. Fowl soup boiled hens, roast ducks, salt pork, plum pudding, always mashed potatoes, cheese wine almonds raisins & figs. Crossing the American line W— wind.

13th Day very bad. Breakst *Pigs fry*, meaning liver lights &c. fried together—cold beef. Dinner. Cold round, pease soup, curried pork & rice, Rhubarb pudding.

14th Potato & fish beat together called here twice laid, to breakst Hen soup & fried tripe, rice pudding. High wind 200 miles south of Farewell. Pickled leg of pork, pease pudding, Cherry pie. Longi 43 & 16. Wind right ahead close reefed topsails & no mizzen. Other ship lost part of her rigging.

15th Breakst Ham & egg— Dinner pease soup, roast pork currant pudding no observation. Mrs Fin^n ill & Miss Allan also in bed Miss Ross rheumatism & I all sore sitting on wood bottomed chairs.

16th *Portable* soup Pillau (hens pork rice mixed) a round of beef, suet pud^g

17th Lob scones to breakst Irish stew, salt fish fried tripe & pancakes. Wind aft. stormy. Long^t 48— On deck for an hour very cold. Har^v has been ill yester^y & today. Spoke to the D^r.

18th Rather better but he did not come to breakfast. Porridge treacle, 2ce [twice] laid. Dinner salt beef pease soup, fried tripe.

LETITIA HARGRAVE, *The Letters of Letitia Hargrave*,
ed. Margaret Macleod, 1947

Nothing comes amiss to sailors in the way of eatables . . . The rank, oily, disgustingly high-scented sea-birds that were caught by the passengers, were all begged and eaten by the crew. One day a very large gull or albatross was handed over to them, and duly demolished . . . When the bird came on deck, quantities of pure oil poured from its beak . . . and on someone's enquiring how it tasted, a steerage passenger very gravely declared it to be 'very like partridge'.

LOUISA MEREDITH, *Notes and Sketches of New South Wales*, 1844

[May 22, 1845] Steerage very sickly . . . Children in the Small Pox become rapidly worse; as yet, no other positive cases appear, though several are suspected . . . [a] child dangerously ill of inflammation of the chest. *No leeches on board.* Many suffering from rheumatic pains and gatherings in the ear . . . Conversed with a very respectable woman who, with her child, was walking on the deck. 'Oh! Madam', said she, 'we suffer terribly from want of room and comfort. Sometimes we cannot cook, for all the fires are put out by the spray, and the wind, and the rain, and we have nothing to warm and nourish us after this dreadful sickness.'

SARAH MYTTON MAURY, *An Englishwoman in America*, 1848

There were not many deaths among big people [adults], only one man and four women, and the man and two of the women were sick before they came, and another one died in the family way, and another went overboard on washing-day.

Letters from Highland Emigrants, [1853]

The Captain smokes out the steerage passengers if they do not emerge on a fine day . . .

ANNE ISABELLA SMITH, *Diary on board the 'Finland'*, 1848

The greatest and most injurious inconvenience is, that the modesty of English women too frequently restrains them from relieving themselves by going to the usual place for the purpose, which place is, and must be, upon the deck, and within sight of all those who are upon the deck. This reluctance, however amiable in itself (and very amiable it is), has often produced very disagreeable, not to say fatal consequences. French women are excellent sailors, but English women, and American women, must change their natures before this can cease to be a subject of really serious importance. Use every argument in your power to get over this difficulty with regard to your wife, and lose no opportunity of overcoming her scruples.

WILLIAM COBBETT, *The Emigrant's Guide*, 1829

There were occasionally more obvious dangers to be met with, too, before the voyage out ended and the journey onwards began.

A dark and starless night closed in, accompanied by cold winds and drizzling rain. We seemed to have made a sudden leap from the torrid to the frigid zone. Two hours before, my light summer clothing was almost insupportable, and now a heavy and well-lined plaid formed but an inefficient screen from the inclemency of the weather. After watching for some time the singular effect produced by the lights in the town reflected in the water, and weary with a long day of anticipation and excitement, I made up my mind to leave the deck and retire to rest. I had just settled down my baby in her berth, when the vessel struck, with a sudden crash that sent a shiver through her whole frame. Alarmed, but not aware of the real danger that hung over us, I groped my way to the cabin, and thence ascended to the deck.

Here a scene of confusion prevailed that baffles description. By some strange fatality, the *Horsley Hill* had changed her position, and run foul of us in the dark. The *Anne* was a small brig, and her unlucky neighbour a heavy three-masted vessel, with three hundred Irish emigrants on board; and as her bowsprit was directly across the bows of the *Anne*, and she anchored, and unabled to free herself from the deadly embrace, there was no small danger of the poor brig going down in the unequal struggle.

Unable to comprehend what was going on, I raised my head above the companion ladder, just at the critical moment when the vessels were grappled together. The shrieks of the women, the shouts and oaths of the men, and the barking of the dogs in either ship, aided the dense darkness of the night in producing a most awful and stunning effect.

'What is the matter?' I gasped out. 'What is the reason of this dreadful confusion?'

The captain was raging like a chafed bull, in the grasp of several frantic women, who were clinging, shrieking, to his knees.

With great difficulty I persuaded the women to accompany me below. The mate hurried off with the cabin light upon the deck, and we were left in total darkness to await the result.

A deep, strange silence fell upon my heart. It was not exactly fear, but a sort of nerving of my spirit to meet the worst. The cowardly behaviour of my companions inspired me with courage. I was ashamed of their pusillanimity and want of faith in the Divine Providence. I sat down, and calmly begged them to follow my example.

An old woman, called Williamson, a sad reprobate, in attempting to do so, set her foot within the fender, which the captain had converted into a repository for empty glass bottles; the smash that ensued was echoed by a shriek from the whole party.

'God guide us,' cried the ancient dame; 'but we are going into eternity. I shall be lost; my sins are more in number than the hairs of my head.' This confession was followed by oaths and imprecations too blasphemous to repeat . . .

'Mrs Moodie, we are lost,' said Margaret Williamson, the youngest daughter of the old woman, a pretty girl, who had been the belle of the ship, flinging herself on her knees before me, and grasping both my hands in hers. 'Oh, pray for me! pray for me! I cannot, I dare not, pray for myself; I was never taught prayer.' Her voice was choked with convulsive sobs, and scalding tears fell in torrents from her eyes over my hands. I never witnessed such an agony of despair. Before I could say one word to comfort her, another shock seemed to lift the vessel upwards. I felt my own blood run cold, expecting instantly to go down; and thoughts of death, and the unknown eternity at our feet, flitted vaguely through my mind.

'If we stay here, we shall perish,' cried the girl, springing to her feet. 'Let us go on deck, mother, and take our chance with the rest.'

'Stay,' I said; 'you are safer here. British sailors never leave women to perish. You have fathers, husbands, brothers on board, who will not forget you. I beseech you to remain patiently here until the danger is past.' I might as well have preached to the winds. The headstrong creatures would no longer be controlled. They rushed simultaneously upon deck, just as the *Horsley Hill* swung off, carrying with her part of the outer frame of our deck and the larger portion of our stern. When tranquillity was restored, fatigued both in mind and body, I sunk into a profound sleep, and did not awake until the sun had risen high above the wave-encircled fortress of Quebec.

SUSANNA MOODIE, *Roughing it in the Bush*, 1852

The wagon was lined with green cloth, to make it pleasant and soft for the eye, with three or four large pockets on each side, to hold many little conveniences,—looking-glasses, combs, brushes, and so on. Mr Frink bought, in Cincinnati, a small sheet-iron cooking-stove, which was lashed on behind the wagon. To prepare for crossing the deserts, we also had two India-rubber bottles holding five gallons each, for carrying water.

Our outfit for provisions was plenty of hams and bacon, covered with care from the dust, apples, peaches, and preserved fruits of different kinds, rice, coffee, tea, beans, flour, corn-meal, crackers, sea-biscuit, butter, and lard. The canning of fruits had not been invented yet—at least not in the west, so far as we knew.

MARGARET FRINK, *Journal*, 1897

We found ourselves again travelling through a rich pasturage country, abounding with the most enchanting, charming scenery that had greeted us since we had left the 'Big Bend'. We came into 'Ta Bac' with better spirits, and more vigorous teams, than was allowed us during the last few hundred miles.

At this place, one of our number became the unwilling subject of a most remarkable, and dampening transaction. Mrs M. . . . while bearing her two hundred and forty of avoirdupois about the camp at rather a too rapid rate, suddenly came in sight of a well that had been dug years before, by the Mexican settlers.

While guiding her steps so as to shun this huge looking hole, suddenly she felt old earth giving way beneath her. It proved that a well of more ancient date than the one she was seeking to shun, had been dug directly in her way, but had accumulated a fine covering of grass during the lapse of years. The members of the camp who were lazily whiling away the hours on the down hill side of the well's mouth, were soon apprised of the fact some *momentous* cause had interfered with nature's laws, and had opened some new and hitherto unseen fountains in her bosom. With the sudden disappearance of Mrs M., there came a large current of clear cold water flowing through the camp, greatly dampening our joys, and starting us upon the alert to inquire into the cause of this strange phenomenon. Mrs M., we soon found safely lodged in the old well, but perfectly secure, as the water, on the principle that no two opaque bodies can occupy the same space at the same time,—had leaped out, as Mrs M.'s mammoth proportions had suddenly laid an imperative possessory injunction upon the entire dimensions of 'the hole in the ground.'

MARY OATMAN, *Life Among the Indians*, 1857

This part of the road was the most unpleasant part of the journey, for the alkali was so thick that it formed a perfect crust, which, for miles, looked as white as snow. Our hands and lips were so sore from it. Such a dust as would raise as we traveled along. We would be so covered when we stopped at nightfall that we could not tell our nearest neighbours, as all looked alike.

MARGARET WHITE CHAMBERS, *Reminiscences*, 1903

One of the most wonderful sights on these desolate plains was the mirage. The first time this strange phenomenon appeared I was filled with astonishment. While riding one day along the monotonous level road and gazing ahead at the wide expanse of sand and sage brush, a peculiarly dazzling and brilliant light appeared like sunlight on the water. My first impression was that we were approaching a lake . . . As I looked, this seemed to change, and a number of buildings came into view, but all upside down, and while still gazing at them they slowly faded from my vision.

LAVINIA HONEYMAN PORTER, *By Ox Team to California*, 1910

'At last the storm came, and the snow fell—I think it must have been at least five or six inches deep within half an hour. The wind was very keen and cutting, and it drifted the snow right into our faces; and thus blinded by the storm, and scarcely able to stand, we stumbled on that day for fully sixteen miles. What we suffered it would be useless for me to attempt to describe. Some of the scenes we witnessed were heartrending.

'There was a young girl, with whom I was very well acquainted, and whom I saw struggling in the snow, clinging to one of the hand-carts, and vainly trying to help in pushing it on, but really doing just the contrary. She is now in Salt Lake City, a helpless cripple, her limbs downwards having been frozen during that storm, and subsequently amputated. A poor old woman, too, whom I think you must have known in London, lingered behind later in the day. When night came on it was impossible for any one to go back to search for her, but, in the morning, not very far from the camp, some torn rags—the remains of her dress—were found, a few bones, a quantity of hair, and at a little distance a female skull, well gnawed, and with the marks of the wolf-fangs still wet upon it;—the snow all round was crimsoned with blood . . . [A] thick heavy mantle of snow covered all the camp; but we contrived to communicate with each other, and soon it was whispered that five poor creatures had been found dead in the tents. Want, and weariness, and the bitter cold, had done their work, and we did not weep for them—they were at rest; but for ourselves we wept that we were left behind—and we looked at one another, wistfully, wondering which of us would be taken next . . . I cannot tell you more now, but I may as well add that when we left Iowa City we were about five hundred in all. Some left us on the way. When we left Florence, and began the journey across the Plains, we were over four hundred and twenty, of which number we buried sixty-seven—a sixth of the whole. The company which followed us, and to which I have frequently alluded, fared worse than we. They numbered six hundred when they started, but they buried one hundred and fifty on the journey—one in every four. May God grant that I may never again see such a sight as was presented by the miserable remnant of that last company as they came on slowly through the Cañon towards Salt Lake Valley.'

FANNY STENHOUSE, *An Englishwoman in Utah*, 1880

From the border of Usoga, where we crossed the Nile into Uganda, we had a sort of triumphal progress; crowds escorting us through each district of a sub-chief, and only parting from us when we passed on to the clutches of a similar crowd waiting; while letters of welcome from the capital kept arriving by the hand of weary and perspiring runners. For the last two days it became quite difficult at times to make our way . . .

On the actual day of our arrival the Bishop had issued a command: 'Miss Browne and Miss Chadwick to remain in their carrying chairs.' Now we two, the juniors, had almost done without these chairs throughout the journey; partly, no doubt, from pride and naughtiness of heart; partly because, having been re-inforced with iron to make them stand the long journey, the chairs were really very heavy and we did not care about being carried in them and only [called them up] occasionally to help us cross a stream (we were more frequently just picked up by the nearest porter and carried across).

So on that last morning, with this edict sent out, there was some difficulty in manning the chairs. Miss Browne was provided some-how. The men who were left for me staggered along for a few miles then gave up. Mr Wright had nobly stayed by me when everyone else of our party was out of sight, and by his words, eight or ten stalwart Bagandas seized and hoisted the chair, and we made a state entry of our own nearly two hours behind the rest of the procession . . .

Then, after an almost delirious (though teetotal) lunch, we were escorted up to the crowded ring of school-houses which encircled the Cathedral, because the crowds would not disperse without seeing us at close quarters. With some difficulty a narrow aisle was cleared down the middle, and we slowly filed through, caught by eager hands on either side, nearly deafened by their tumultuous greetings, trying to get out a carefully-learned word or two in answer . . . Christians, heathen, Mohammedans, all were for once gathered together to welcome 'the five mamas'.

JANE CHADWICK, Memoirs [n.d.]

Arrival, at last.

THREE

FIRST IMPRESSIONS

There are no ghosts in Canada. The country is too new for ghosts.
Susanna Moodie, *Roughing it in the Bush*, 1852

For Mrs Moodie, arriving in Canada in 1832 (along with some fifty thousand other emigrant pioneers driven by hope or despair that year alone), a sense of precedent—even the odd ghost or two—would have been a great comfort. She had answered the advertisements promising grants of land and an honest, homespun fortune to those who were unafraid of work and the wilderness, and, one long, apprehensive voyage later, had found herself suddenly marooned. The Moodies' allotted demesne on the shores of Lake Ontario had never before been settled. There was not even a road to lead them there: they must clear their way as they went. The notion that this place had no history—no familiar, human history, that is—was surprisingly chilling to Susanna. She had not reckoned on being quite so literally a pioneer.

Even the fact that such astounding numbers of Europeans were swarming to the shores of Canada with her did not help much. It was such a vast land, its tracts of water and wild woodland like a giant and indecipherable mosaic; it swelled, blowsy and oppressive, in the fly-ridden summer and then contracted, astringent, tight, and icily cruel, for the rest of the year. It absorbed emigrants and their hopes, until you would hardly know they were there at all.

Susanna, you will gather, was a somewhat reluctant settler. Her first impression of Canada lasted, she said, for years—after which, incidentally, the family prospered, multiplied, and flourished.

31

Other emigrant women shared this frightened awareness of utter unfamiliarity. Their first impressions were understandably tainted by it, and by the after-effects of the voyage out, with its possible legacy in some cases, of sickness or even bereavement. Some, like Jane Chadwick arriving in Uganda at the end of the previous chapter, were delighted with the novelty of it all, but most of the following writers—initially, anyway—found their reactions on disembarking and taking in the surroundings tempered by naivety and disillusionment, and a bleak realization that the long-awaited future, supposed to be so promising, was suddenly here. Now.

Adelaide, Gouger Street
28th January 1840

My dear Parents,

I have very melancholy accounts to give, which I cannot do without great excitement to my feelings.

We landed at Holdfast Bay, about 7 miles from Adelaide (the ship being too large to go into port) on the 10th of December 1839, having been just four months to a day on the Great Deep. We had a safe, and many would say, a delightful voyage; but as regards myself, for the first five weeks I was scarcely able to move my head from my pillow with Sea-sickness, which brought me so low that I could render but very little assistance to the dear children, as I was obliged to be helped on deck by two persons . . . and the children suffered but little from sickness. But as we entered on a warmer climate, the dear children became relaxed (with the exception of Emily) gradually getting weaker and, for want of proper nourishment, became at last sorrowful spectacles to behold. They could eat none of the ship's provisions and our vessel was not like many that are sent out, provided with one or more cows for the accommodation of the sick; and, had I the voyage to take again, I would make that a first consideration as I firmly believe that the dear children would have lived, and much sickness been spared, had we experienced proper attention from our Doctor and been provided with a little natural nourishment.

Poor little Alfred was the first that died on 30th of Oct, and on the 8th of Nov, dear Fanny went and three days after, on the 11th, the dear babe was taken from me. I scarcely know how I sustained the shock, though I was certain they could not recover, yet when poor Fanny went it over-powered me and from the weakness of my frame, reduced me to such a low nervous state that, for many weeks, I was not expected to survive. It seems I gave much trouble but knew nothing about it and, though I was quite conscious that the dear baby and Fanny were thrown overboard, I would still persist that the water could not retain them and that they were with me in the berth. I took strange fancies into my head and thought that Mother had said I should have her nice easy chair to sit up in and, if they would only lift me into it, I would soon get well. I had that chair of Mother's in my 'mind's eye' for many weeks and was continually talking about it.

I was bled and blistered, or rather, plastered, and continued in that weak state until within a week of landing. I think I never should have recovered at Sea—you can have no idea of the effect the sea has upon some constitutions. Mine, for instance. It was a sort of Sea Consumption. Our Captain took great notice of our children, when he saw them gradually wasting away and would send for them into his Cabin and give them port-wine, almost daily. In fact, wine and water was the only nourishment they took for weeks and that was given them too late. I would advise everyone who came out for Australia to bring nourishing things with them and take in turn with what is allowed on board, for the change is so great and so sudden to what we have been accustomed that the constitution, unless very strong, sickens under it.

My dear Emily now seems more precious to us than ever, and I feel very thankful I did not leave her in England. Her health is not as good as formerly, having something Scurvy, the effects of Salt diet. She is also troubled with weak eyes, a complaint exceedingly common in this town, from the great degree of heat, light and dust.

MRS MOGER, *Letter*, 1840

We finally landed in New York [in 1861] all safe and sound and went to a place called Castle Garden, where all the emigrants landed, and where all the freight unloaded from the vessels was brought for storage temporarily. Castle Garden was located at the Battery, just across from the Goddess of Liberty, where the Aquarium is now. It was right on the water front.

Castle Garden was the dumping ground for all kinds of cargo, and it was also crowded with emigrants. The floor was greasy and dirty. Here we had to make our beds on the floor, as did all the other emigrants. Mother spread out the quilts and bedding, and we all lay down in a row, the children, and mother and father. My little brother was sleeping next to me on the dirty floor. There were sacks of brown sugar at our heads. In the night, he awoke and whispered to me, 'Alma, there is a hole in the corner of this sack and I am going to have some of the brown sugar.' We had not had any sugar or candy all the way over, so we got a spoon out of the box and had all the brown sugar we could eat. In the morning we were so sick! We got up, went to the bay and threw it all up, and did not care for any brown sugar after that!

From New York City we traveled by boat up the Hudson, and took the trains at Albany to travel to Omaha, the outfitting place for our trip across the plains. All of us Mormon emigrants were forced to travel on sheep cars, so filthy with sheep beans on the floor that we could not even sit down, and had to stand all the way. We traveled this distance without a change of cars.

ALMA E. M. FELT, *Memoirs*, *c*.1920

We found lying here his Majesty's armed tender The Supply, with her lower masts both out of repair; they were so bad, that she was obliged to have others made of the wood of the country, which was procured with great difficulty, several hundred trees being cut down without finding any sufficiently sound at the core . . . also, The Mary-Anne, a transport-ship, that had been sent out alone, with only women-convicts and provisions on-board.

A dreadful mortality had taken place on-board of most of the transports which had been sent to this country; the poor miserable objects that were landed died in great numbers, so that they were soon reduced to at least *one third* of the number that quitted England.

MARY ANN PARKER, *A Voyage Round the World*, 1795

This is a Government asylum, established as a respectable refuge for all those emigrants from England who may not have succeeded in obtaining employment immediately after landing; and it is also used as a sort of almshouse or workhouse for those old people who may have fallen into poverty, and for whom Government aid has become indispensable. Purists in language insist upon calling this building the Immigrants' Home, whilst others, who remember that its especial purpose is to provide a shelter for those new-comers who have not as yet been able to convert themselves into dwellers in the new country, in any useful sense of the term, but are still as waifs and strays cast upon its shore, consider that Emigrant's Home is the more legitimate title for the abode of those unlucky exports from England who have not at once been able to obtain admission into the human circulation of the new country, but are still, as it were, in store at the place of landing . . .

We are shown into a long room, divided off into separate spaces by wooden partitions, each space being of good size, and doing duty as a private apartment, but much resembling the loose boxes in a nobleman's hunting stable. These represented unfurnished lodgings for the immigrants, some of whom, perhaps, would, if the spaces had contained more accommodation, have bestirred themselves but slowly in seeking independent homes of their own. The place was perfectly clean and well ventilated, and plenty of water was at hand in the yard of the building, a great comfort with the thermometer at 90° as it then was. There was also no lack of water in the form of tears as we went in, for a poor old Irishwoman, whom we found sitting on the floor, with her feet straight out before her and her back against the wall, just as we had often seen her sitting on deck resting against the bulwarks, was crying grievously, in company with her daughter. When we learned the reason for all this lamentation we did not wonder that they were both disconsolate. The poor souls had come out to Swan River intending to proceed

35

from thence, believing it to be a very easy trip, to join the husband and father in Melbourne; and they now found themselves in Australia with almost less chance of getting to Melbourne, in their penniless condition, than if they had remained in London.

MRS EDWARD MILLETT, *An Australian Parsonage*, 1872

Already we had been in the vessel twenty-four hours [from St. Louis], when just at nightfall it stopped: a little boat was lowered into the water, and we were invited to collect our luggage and descend into it, as we were at Phillip's Ferry. We were utterly confounded: there was no appearance of a landing place, no luggage yard, nor even a building of any kind in sight; we however attended to our directions and in a few minutes saw ourselves standing by the brink of the river, bordered by a dark wood, with no-one near to notice us or tell us where we might procure accommodation or find harbour . . . It was in the middle of November, and already very frosty. My husband and I looked at each other until we burst into tears, and our children observing our disquietude began to cry bitterly. Is this America, thought I?

After my husband was gone to find help I caused my four eldest children to sit together on one of our beds, covered them from the cold as well as I could, and endeavoured to pacify them . . . Above me was the chill blue canopy of heaven, a wide river before me, and a dark wood behind.

REBECCA BURLEND, *A True Picture of Emigration* [1848]

The Burlend family was one of many tempted abroad by the fat promises of various emigration schemes only to find that they had parted with their relatives, their home, and their money, for absolutely nothing. Emigration became less a matter of business speculation for them than of basic survival. And survival depended on work.

A gentleman returned [to the ship] this evening bringing us information worth receiving. He had met a person in the city who enquired of him if we had a miller on board among our passengers, as he knew a party very much in want of one as they were scarce folks in Sydney. He told him he believed there was one and only one on board. He said he should feel very much obliged if he would send him. His employer would give him one hundred and four pounds a year with rations sufficient for himself and wife and likewise a house to live in. The news seemed really too good to be true. I could hardly bring my mind to believe it. Fortune actually coming out of Sydney to meet us. I could not sleep a wink all night for thinking. It appeared like a dream, I was unable to interpret much less believe. Thursday October 27th a lovely day. Thomas started first thing this morning in quest of his new situation. I spent a very anxious day as to the upshot of this unlooked for affair. A gentleman returned about tea time with a message from Thomas to say that he could not return until the following morning as he had to go to Parramatta, sixteen miles out of Sydney to be engaged and would not be able to get any conveyance back that evening.

Friday, October 28th a most exquisite day, my anxiety seems increased two fold. This morning Thomas returned about six in the morning bringing intelligence that he was engaged at the rate of one hundred and four pounds a year with board, lodging and firing found us. The place intended for our future home is two hundred miles from Sydney named Yass, a station half way to the Ovens diggings. We are to leave Sydney tomorrow by the Mail which starts at five in the evening, the fare is seven guineas each without luggage. We leave that behind to be sent by the bullock drays after us which takes a month and sometimes three to reach their destination. Mr Hardy, for that is our employer's name, has agreed to pay our expenses by the mail, the luggage we have to pay for ourselves. I feel very timid at the thoughts of going up the country such a distance particularly there having been a most brutal murder just committed there which you have doubtless heard of in the papers. The man now lies in Goulburn Jail awaiting his trial. However, there was no alternative so [I] made up my mind to it in the best way I could.

ISABELLA HERCUS, *Journal from Gravesend to Sydney*, 1853

Positive thinking like Isabella's was a valuable asset: the emigrant's alchemy, transforming the most dismal of prospects.

Tuesday 23 March, 1841. Barque *Parkfield*. We breakfasted at 8 to start at 9 for Australind. The weather was most lovely and a fair Irish breeze carried us up quickly to the encampment. The scenery of the estuary gratified us extremely; the banks on each side beautifully wooded down to the water's edge, with foliage of varied tints even at this season of the year. Mama was charmed.

On arriving at the tents we were most warmly received by Mrs Austen and were astonished at the comfort and neatness of her tent. Fruit, wine, home-made bread and cakes were laid for us, and most refreshing and delicious we found that which we had so long desired to taste—good bread. The appearance of the camp struck us much; the tents distributed under large, spreading trees, a hill covered with wood and bush rising behind. I never saw a more picturesque scene.

LOUISA CLIFTON, *Diary*, 1840–1

Mr —— was very kind, and spoke in raptures of the woods, which formed the theme of conversation during our journey—their beauty, their vastness, the comfort and independence enjoyed by those who had settled in them; and he so inspired me with the subject that I did nothing all day but sing as we rode along—'A life in the woods for me,' until we came to the woods . . .

Here succeeded a long pause, during which friend Tom seemed mightily tickled with his reminiscences, for he leaned back in his chair and gave way to loud, hollow bursts of laughter . . .

'The Woods! Ha! ha! When I used to be roaming through those woods, shooting—though not a thing could I ever find to shoot, for birds and beasts are not such fools as our English emigrants—and I chanced to think of you coming to spend the rest of your lives in the woods—I used to stop, and hold my sides, and laugh until the woods rang again. It was the only consolation I had.'

SUSANNA MOODIE, *Roughing it in the Bush*, 1852

Strange lands. Strange customs, too.

[Petersburg:] My passport is somewhere being examined. To-morrow I have to go before the Secret Police, in case, I suppose, of misdemeaning myself at some future period. My books, too, are not yet come back from the Board of Censor . . . Russia is nothing to England, nothing at all—paper and gingerbread!

A LADY, *Russian Chit-Chat*, 1856

Our entrance to Marand was distinguished by a most disagreeable ceremony, which was attempted to be repeated at every village at which we halted, not only on this but on every succeeding journey during our residence in Persia. On approaching the town, I observed an unfortunate cow in the midst of the crowd, close to the roadside, held down by the head and feet; when we came within a yard or so of the miserable animal, a man brandished a large knife, with which he instantly, before there was time for interference, severed its head from its body. He then ran across our road with the head, allowing the blood to flow on our path in torrents, and we passed on to encounter a repetition of the same cruel rites performed on various sheep. This ceremony was called Korbān, or sacrifice, these poor creatures having been immolated in order that all the misfortunes, evils, and disasters, which might overtake us, should fall on them; and fall on them they assuredly did.

LADY SHEIL, *Glimpses of Life . . . in Persia*, 1856

[On our first day] Archdeacon Walker let off a bombshell. 'You must all sit down now and write an order for a year's groceries, clothes, everything else you may want in eighteen months' time'. And when we exclaimed, he explained that the returning caravan would only rest for one whole day; they would take our letters back so all must be written as soon as possible, and this mail would take about six months to reach home, while the goods ordered might

39

take a year in coming out, so whatever we were provided with in our outfit must last for that time.

JANE CHADWICK, *Memoirs* [n.d.]

New York is hell upon earth for young persons, particularly women, taking a moral view of it; it is the greatest den of iniquity in existence; believe nothing else.

Sidney's Emigrant's Journal, 1848

Broadway is a perfect puzzle. How smaller and lighter crafts make undemolished way through that throng of omnibuses, is amazing. Many a street in London is as much crowded, but I do not suppose in any one, if you except the vicinity of the Crystal Palace at evening, you could count twenty omnibuses at a time within sight. Yet there is no pressing and driving—but cheerful, smiling courtesy on all hands . . . Not one tipsy shout—not one staggering mortal—no wife or sister looking fearfully on her escort. Ah, Scotland! When will temperance do for thee what it has done for these crowded cities!

ANON. [MARY LUNDIE], *America As I Found It*, 1852

The most striking first impressions—especially of native peoples—were informed by ignorance, sometimes of quite virtuosic proportion.

The ladies, in my opinion, take precedence of the other sex, both in virtue and talent. They furnish a noble instance of moral integrity in preserving themselves uncontaminated amidst the drinking propensities of their degraded lords—the one acting as a foil to display the purity of the other . . . With respect to the opposite sex, they may be patriots, they may be brave . . . and they may be enterprising and persevering, but certainly they are far from being amiable.

MRS FELTON, *Life in America*, 1838

We are all sick of church & churchmen & are going it very strong with the Methodists, who assuredly give us plenty of buttering if they cannot get up genuine gratitude. I don't deny that *we* are anxious to get a good word even from Wesleyans, for no Episcopalian has come who has not reviled the Co^y for every thing that was execrable. They may for what I know be right in most things but one, viz. the maltreating of the Indians, they are very far wrong, & they must know it too. For in summer the Indians are employed out of charity & till the ship arrives it is ludicrous to see a band of 15 or 16 with their spades or whatever they are using lying beside them & they all squat on their faces asleep. This is in the forenoon, at night they either work in their own way, though Alec w^d do it better, with their pipes in their mouths, or else they sit chattering or gambling, of which they are very fond, till the bell rings, & up they jump & run as hard as they can in a long string along the platform to the provision sheds where they get their allowances & go to their tents. There are some curiosities among them. They all say 'Sir' to me, the half-breeds call me 'small Mr Hargrave' I mean the children do, for of course the full grown ones are as good as the whites.

LETITIA HARGRAVE, *The Letters . . .*, ed. Margaret Macleod, 1947

[The Indian's] walk reminds me of our distinguished tragedians as they tread the stage. Like them, he firmly plants the foot, and draws his mantle in folds about him, with the same commanding air of deportment, with this difference: his regal dignity is natural, while theirs is only assumed. He could not have studied them; and it is not probable they have taken a Pottawattamie Indian as their model . . .

It is to be regretted that all efforts have as yet been but partially successful to civilize this benighted race. With minds as susceptible of cultivation as their waste prairies, the light imparted merely tinges the dark surface, to be dispelled when their loved hunting grounds lure them away to assume again the blanket and tomahawk.

CATHERINE STEWART, *New Homes in the West*, 1843

[The Hottentots] are by nature tolerably white, and not unhandsome, but as soon as a child is born, they rub it all over with oil, and lay it in the sun; this they repeat 'till it becomes brown: and always break the infant's nose, so that it lays close to its face.

MRS KINDERSLEY, *Letters . . .*, 1777

The Englishmen who have travelled across this part of the country are comparatively few, and the advent of a white woman is still a remarkable event. When a white-haired old lady landed recently from a private American yacht she aroused greater interest than had been shown in any previous visitor. The natives informed the Commissioner that it had been a great surprise to them to see an old white woman, as they were under the impression that women were destroyed by Europeans after they had passed middle age.

LADY DENHAM in *United Empire*, 1930

There are everywhere in the Towns as I passed, a Number of Indians, the Natives of the Country, and are the most salvage [*sic*] of all the salvages of that kind that I had ever Seen . . . They have in some places Landes of their owne, and [are] Govern'd by Law's of their own making;—they marry many wives and at pleasure put them away, and on ye least dislike or fickle humour, on either side, saying *Stand away* to one another is a sufficient Divorce. And indeed those uncomely *Stand aways* are too much in Vogue among the English in this Indulgent Colony . . . and that on very trivial matters of which some have been told me, but are not proper to be Retold by a Female pen, tho' some of that foolish sex have had too large a share in the story.

MADAM KNIGHT, *The Journals . . . 1704*, 1825

I asked one of the Herrenhut brethren whether there were any *real* Hottentots, and he said, 'Yes, one;' and next morning, as I sat waiting for early prayers under the big oak-trees in the Plaats (square), he came up, followed by a tiny old man hobbling along with a long stick to support him. 'Here', said he, 'is the *last* Hottentot; he is a hundred and seven years old, and lives all alone.' I looked on the little, wizened, yellow face, and was shocked that he should be dragged up like a wild beast to be stared at. A feeling of pity which felt like remorse fell upon me, and my eyes filled as I rose and stood before him, so tall and like a tyrant and oppressor, while he uncovered his poor little old snow-white head, and peered up in my face. I led him to the seat, and helped him to sit down, and said in Dutch, 'Father, I hope you are not tired; you are old.' He saw and heard as well as ever, and spoke *good* Dutch in a firm voice. 'Yes, I am above a hundred years old, and alone—quite alone.' I sat beside him, and he put his head on one side, and looked curiously up at me with his faded, but still piercing, little wild eyes. Perhaps he had a perception of what I felt—yet I hardly think so; perhaps he thought I was in trouble, for he crept close up to me, and put one tiny brown paw into my hand, which he stroked with the other, and asked (like most coloured people) if I had children. I said, 'Yes, at home in England'; and he patted my hand again, and said, 'God bless them!' It was a relief to feel that he was pleased, for I should have felt like a murderer if my curiosity had added a moment's pain to so tragic a face.

LADY LUCIE DUFF GORDON, *Letters from the Cape*, 1864

Despite the grave reservations of Lady Lucie, and Susanna Moodie's more temporary ones in the next extract, the company of one's own kind was many an exiled emigrant's greatest solace.

It was four o'clock when we landed on the rocks, which the rays of an intensely scorching sun had rendered so hot that I could scarcely place my foot upon them. How the people without shoes bore it, I cannot imagine. Never shall I forget the extraordinary spectacle that met our sight . . . A crowd of many hundred Irish emigrants had been landed during the present and former day; and all this motley crew—men, women, and children, who were not confined by sickness to the sheds (which greatly resembled cattle-pens)—were employed in washing clothes, or spreading them out on the rocks and bushes to dry.

The men and boys were *in* the water, while the women, with their scanty garments tucked above their knees, were trampling their bedding in tubs, or in holes in the rocks, which the retiring tide had left half full of water. Those who did not possess washing-tubs, pails, or iron pots, or could not obtain access to a hole in the rocks, were running to and fro, screaming and scolding in no measured terms. The confusion of Babel was among them . . . We were literally stunned by the strife of tongues. I shrank, with feelings almost akin to fear, from the hard-featured, sun-burnt harpies, as they elbowed rudely past me.

I had heard and read much of savages, and have since seen, during my long residence in the bush, somewhat of uncivilized life; but the Indian is one of Nature's gentlemen—he never says or does a rude or vulgar thing. The vicious, uneducated barbarians who form the surplus of over-populous European countries, are far behind the wild man in delicacy of feeling or natural courtesy.

SUSANNA MOODIE, *Roughing it in the Bush*, 1852

There were about eighty men at Ebuta Metta, but no women at all. Occasionally an intrepid wife appears for a few months to gladden her husband's heart . . . [b]ut as a rule the men do their own housekeeping, and live in single blessedness, more or less. They seem to get on quite nicely without us, and certainly lack none of the creature comforts. They give each other frequent and elaborate dinners, preceded by 'small chop' [?small talk] and cocktails on the veranda, and wind up with bridge and whisky pegs in the small hours of the morning. They have tennis courts and golf links, curtains and cushions, the latest books, and an occasional piano. There is only one thing that they sadly need, and that is a nice pink lampshade.

MRS HORACE TREMLETT, *With the Tin Gods*, 1915

A weary afternoon, evening, and night, succeeded each other, and were succeeded in their turn by a still wearier morning and afternoon. I constantly asked the boatmen how much farther it was to Langat, but they did not appear to know exactly. Sometimes they told me it was so many tanjongs (bends of the river) off; but when I had counted that number go by, they said they had been mistaken, and it was more tanjongs still. If I asked how many more? I received the unfailing Malay answer. 'Tidak tŭntu'—'It is not certain.' At last, when in despair I had given up asking them, I was informed Langat was in sight. Soon we arrived at the landing-place before mentioned, and having reached terra firma as well as limbs stiffened by twenty-four hours of oubliette would allow, I walked towards the house. Mr Innes had had no notice of my coming, as postal arrangements there were none in the country, but a boatman ran on ahead to tell him, and he came out to meet us.

The house was worse than I had expected.

EMILY INNES, *The Chersonese with the Gilding Off*, 1885

I shall never forget the look my mother turned upon the place. Without a word she crossed its threshold, and standing very still, looked slowly around her. Then something within her seemed to give way, and she sank upon the ground . . . When she finally took it in she buried her face in her hands, and in that way she sat for

hours without moving or speaking . . . Never before had we seen
our mother give way to despair.

ANNA SHAW, *The Story of a Pioneer*, 1915

I must now give you some description of our hut. In the first place
it has two rooms which occupy the space of your wash-house. Each
of these rooms have a window, only think three panes across and
two high. The bedroom you must understand has been in the wars
for three squares out of the six have got board in them instead of
glass which is not quite so transparent. The sitting room has two
boarded up which of course outside in particular gives the place a
very respectable appearance. Wood being rather a scarce article
here they cannot afford to board the rooms. Our bedroom has one
of Nature's own making—the mother earth. Now I hope you will
not laugh for as Thomas used to say, you might be took to yourself,
but of all the bedsteads you ever saw I warrant you will never come
across one to match ours. It is one of our own contriving and erect-
ing and a four post too. Thomas went out and dug up four old
clumsy stakes belonging to a fence. He brought them home; he
then dug four great holes in the bedroom. We put a post in each
and then rammed the dirt in round them. The next thing to be
thought of was the side and foot pieces. We went and fetched some
more of the poor old fence and nailed them to the posts but we had
to hunt for all our nails before we could do that even. We then
nailed a rough piece of board across for the head-board. The next
consideration was how to contrive a bottom. So after a good deal of
scheming Thomas at last hit upon a plan. He nailed three bars of
wood across and then fetched a large sheet of bark and laid [it]
upon them which answers admirably and we sleep as sound upon a
mattress on a sheet of bark as thousands do upon beds of down. In
our sitting room we have a few odd pieces of board laid down of all
sizes and shapes. Our fire we have upon a hearth. The walls of our
hut are slabs of wood just as they have been split down in the
rough, not even a splinter planed off them. We can see daylight
through every one. They have had mud plastered in between them
but a great deal of it has dropped out so you see our rooms are very

airy. The roof and chimney are made of bark put together in a sort of form—a patch here and a patch there as if the wind had blown them together. Our door, for we have only one, opens with a bobin. We have no water closet; that is a luxury they think folks can do without. Our water we have to fetch half a mile from the river.

ISABELLA HERCUS, *Journal from Gravesend to Sydney*, 1853

English tailors, shoemakers, saddlers, and inn-keepers, hang out their signs in every street; and the preponderance of the English language over every other spoken in the chief streets, would make one fancy it a coast town in Britain . . . The number of pianofortes brought from England is astonishing. There is scarcely a house without one.

MARIA GRAHAM, *Journal of a Residence in Chile*, 1824

I remained in the house during the heat of the day; but after dinner we drove round the race-course, a lonely little peninsula lying beneath the wild high mountains, and hemmed in by the river. Here all the *elite* of the colony assemble for air and exercise of an evening; yet, although in one or two of the perhaps half-dozen equipages on the broad circular path sat a delicate-looking European lady, in short-sleeved white muslin pelisse, long gloves, thin scarf, and transparent bonnet; and a few impatient horses were reined in by white riders, it struck me that the carriage-drive had a very deserted aspect and that our countrymen and countrywomen appeared pale, languid, and dispirited.

ELIZABETH MELVILLE, *A Residence at Sierra Leone*, 1849

The harmattan wind is now blowing, and everything in the house is covered with an impalpable red dust; even our eyes are affected by it . . . Every article of furniture is shrinking and cracking—paper and the boards of books curling up—veneer peeling off—and the strings of the pianoforte breaking. I hear it is much stronger at the Gambia, where it feels like the breath of a hot furnace, causing the panels of doors to shrink and fall out, and glass to become so brittle that it snaps asunder though untouched by any person.

Ibid.

Surely, if anyone could cope in such trying domestic circumstances, it must be a British woman, fabled (in all the emigrant propaganda) for her intrepid and indomitable nature?

The winter had now fairly set in—the iron winter of 1833. The snow was unusually deep, and it being our first winter in Canada, and passed in such a miserable dwelling, we felt it very severely. In spite of all my boasted fortitude—and I think my powers of endurance have been tried to the uttermost since my sojourn in this country—the rigour of the climate subdued my proud, independent, British spirit, and I actually shamed my womanhood, and cried with the cold. Yes, I ought to blush at evincing such unpardonable weakness; but I was foolish and inexperienced, and unaccustomed to the yoke.

SUSANNA MOODIE, *Roughing it in the Bush*, 1852

There was plenty of time to learn.

FOUR

SETTLING IN

Leave the world and its cares all behind—not a sigh
Need ruffle the calm of your breast.
Come, come and enjoy all these pleasures with me,
In the lovely, luxuriant west!
Catherine Stewart, *New Homes in the West,* 1843

A nd Catherine had actually **been** *there and done it: rhap-sodic and somewhat saccharine as it is, this little ditty was not written by a propagandist at home but by a woman who found in the homesteads of America's Midwest her heart's desire.*

Lucky her.

It did happen to others, of course (if a little more prosaically). Once those startling and unfamiliar first impressions had had time to evaporate, and the business of settling in began, emigrant women could either fit in with whatever society and circumstances they found abroad, or else create their own from scratch. They reacted to gentility and brutality (in the company and the landscape alike) according to their previous experience: to the addled Mary Church in Sierra Leone, for example, it was only the singing from missionary chapels that floated over the fetid air at five o'clock in the morning that kept her sane, while Ellen Clacy revelled in the eccentric and rather thrilling chaos of the Australian goldfields. It was all a matter of finding a new context, a new station in life, and existing as comfortably as possible within it.

49

For women, particularly, this context was framed by the home. More sophisticated 'matters domestic' are tackled later on, but there were more basic household duties to perform first. Like constructing the house itself. Mrs Stewart in a North American clearing and Mrs Wilkinson in pungent Zululand speak for others here. Then there is the matter of the neighbours, both imported and home-grown; of coping with the climate, with the local culture, and morality . . . Establishing a home from home abroad, which was most women emigrants' purpose, can very rarely have been the airy-fairy experience Catherine Stewart's poem suggests. Especially when you consider how often that very home from home might shift:

In March, 1836, we left Fleet Street for a lodging in Fish Street, St. Paul's Churchyard. On June 28 we embarked on board the *Africaine* for South Australia. On November 13 we landed at Glenelg and occupied a small tent for about a fortnight. We then removed into a large one, in which we remained about four months. This was then taken down and sent up to Adelaide to serve as a store until one was erected, and the girls and I removed into a rush hut. Mr Thomas was then at Adelaide, and sleeping in the small tent which had been taken there before. From the rush hut we all removed to Adelaide on June 1, 1837, again into a tent hired for us, our own being occupied, as I said before. After some time we removed into another tent, which we purchased, and in September the same year we entered the apartments next to the printing office, which we later left. Our removal into Rhantregwnwyn Cottage makes the ninth time between Ladyday in 1836 and January 1, 1840.

MARY THOMAS, *The Diary*, ed. Evan Kyffin Thomas, 1925

We like this place very well, Allan had 3s. 9d. per day and board; now he is hired for a twelvemonth for 26 pounds. We got places for the girls the day we came here, 15s. per month for Harriet (12 years old) and 10s. for Charlotte (10 years old), they both like their places

well . . . Dear Mother, if you were here, you could get a good cup
of tea, and that large box that Elizabeth give you full of snuff for
½d . . . Dear Sister Mary, if you had come with us, it would have
been the means of making your fortune, you could have seven
dollars per month, one dollar is five shillings english. This is a
good country.

ELIZABETH PUDDOCK in *Emigration: Extracts of Letters
from Settlers*, 1832

*The young Puddocks' salaries were essential to the family's
well-being in Australia. Elsewhere—almost in a different
world—colonial childhoods were more balmily spent.*

On entering a family-house in India, you can scarcely make your
way through toys of every description; every room seems equally a
nursery; dining and drawing rooms, bed and dressing rooms, alike
appear the property of the young people. Each child has one, and
sometimes two attendants, who follow it wherever it goes. The
women are called ayahs; and it is generally a palanquin-boy who
superintends the whole nursery establishment.

On entering, you will find, in the verandah of the house, rock-
ing-horses, carts, low tables and small chairs, in most agreeable
confusion, with drums, swords and sticks, forming a collection
of extraordinary variety. Then the young ladies and gentlemen
themselves contribute no small share to the astonishment of the
stranger. Their dress consists of one single garment, of cotton or
muslin, made scarcely with any sleeve, and reaching a little below
the knee, and they go without shoes and stockings during the
heat of the day. Perhaps, at the time you pay your visit, the gay
romping scene may be varied, by one or two of the youngsters
being asleep; but that does not mean that you are rid of them.
The youngest, a baby from one month to one year old, is being
rocked to sleep on the feet of the ayah. This woman sits down on
the ground, balances the infant's head upon her two feet, with
the child's feet in her lap, and thus rocks her feet backwards and
forwards, like the motion of a cradle, at the same time singing a

monotonous kind of song consisting only of four or five notes, repeated over and over again, adding a few words which mean 'baby, by-by!' At the same time, a little further on, you will see a little one about two years old, lying asleep on a mat upon the ground, with a kind of cage over it formed of bamboo, and covered with green gauze, in shape something resembling a large wire dish-cover; it is always placed over children when they are asleep, to prevent musquitoes and insects of any description disturbing the little slumberer. Children of all ages sleep for two or three hours in the middle of the day. Their dinner forms a distinct meal in the family arrangements, and their comfort is more attended to than that of the elder branches. The young *butchas* are the chief objects of attention; they have their own low table, and each his own chair; they have their small table-cloth and dinner-napkins, and each a silver spoon, fork, and drinking-cup.

Their dinner consists of curry and rice, cutlets made of chicken or mutton, *pish posh*, which is chicken and rice stewed together, and sweet potatoes, which are generally fried, and form a delicious vegetable, and also yams. Then come in the pudding, the plantain fritters, and a little fruit; the latter is very sparingly given, as it is considered very unwholesome for children; toast and water is most generally given them to drink. The servants stand behind their chairs, most frequently two to each child, during the whole meal, and you will hear Miss Eliza, about six years old, cry out 'Boy, why don't you bring the punker? don't you see I am hot, you stupid fellow? Run this moment and put water upon it.' Then master Charles, of four, will be heard exclaiming 'Change my plate, I say, and don't talk there, and bring me a finger-glass; pick up my napkin, sir; don't you see I have dropped it?' In the evening, about five o'clock, begin the dressing of the little party; shoes, stockings, trowsers, frock, all the elegant costume of English children, are fully displayed, and after the heat of the day, they either go out in the carriage with mamma, or walk out, attended by a dozen servants.

MRS MAJOR CLEMONS, *The Manners and Customs of Society in India*, 1841

Someone rapped at the door today. I opened it, and there was a gentleman who informed us he 'was hunting a girl,' to work in his hotel. He had seen so many here he thought we would like to go out to work. With a decided toss of her head Dora told him 'we had not come to *that* yet' and Miss Nan with her nose elevated at an angle of 45 degrees informed him that 'when we wanted a place, we would let him know.' I was more amused than insulted, and said 'I thought six dollars a week pretty good wages, and if the worst came to the worst *I* might go.' He bowed himself out, and after he left I could but think how nice if we could help light our Father's burdens. Of course, there are more ways than in going out to do housework . . .

When mother came in from her walk, the girls told how 'terribly we had been insulted,' and explained it all by our living in this horrid old house.

MOLLIE DORSEY SANFORD, *The Journal . . . 1857–66*, 1976

Family pride was an easily affordable tonic for those in unwontedly reduced circumstances. House pride, too.

I must now tell you the events of the past week, when most unusual business occupied us all. Last Friday was the day fixed for the 'Bee' for raising the frame of our new house. On Thursday Miss Haycock came. She had kindly offered to help our young people with the cooking and other domestic affairs incident upon such an occasion. The young men were also engaged to lend a hand in the great work. All day the kitchen was a busy place, everybody at work making pies and cakes, for it is always expected that if all goes on well and safely the young people who have given their services should have what they call 'a spree.' Miss Caddy, Bessy's great friend, was here too. Everyone was up early enough on Friday morning, our tenants arrived at half-past four o'clock, Mr Charles Dunlop before five, and at six we all sat down to breakfast, fifteen in the parlour and five in the kitchen. The children, except Willie and Frank were still in bed. Before seven o'clock on Friday morning, July 9th, the work was begun; the men first carrying the square logs to the spot where they were to lie. The two sills of the sides were then put down on the stone foundation. They are fifty-six feet long and were all cut ready for the upright pieces to fit in. When these long logs were placed exactly right, the end ones twenty-six feet long were brought over and laid so that the mortised corners should fit when closed. This was accomplished with huge *beetles* (wooden mallets), then the corners were secured by large wooden pins. So far being done they next proceeded to join the *bents* together; of these there were to be six; great square timbers, the upright ones fourteen feet and the cross ones twenty-six feet long. These were mortised together in this form: — ⊓ and laid flat with the ends nearly over the holes into which they were to fit. This all occupied some hours and dinner was called at half-past twelve.

Everything was ready to begin 'to raise' after dinner; just before noon two of the Reids and two of Captain Bray's sons arrived.

We had a famous dinner, substantial though not very elegant; most of it was cold as our cooking apparatus does not admit of doing much at once, and besides, as the hour depended on circumstances, we thought cold meats would be the best. However we had a roast pig and a boiled leg of mutton, a dish of fish, a large cold mutton pie, cold ham and cold roast mutton, mashed potatoes and beans and carrots; sixteen people sat down in the parlour, six in the kitchen, and in another room a table was set for the children (our own six boys, Michael Haycock and Henry Reid). For second course we had a large rice pudding, a large bread and butter pudding, and currant and gooseberry tarts.

After dinner the young men saw clouds rising so would not delay a minute. And now began the work of *raising*. They went to the upper end of the first *bent* and raised it as high as they could with their hands, then eight men took long poles with a spike in the end of each and steadily raised up the great heavy frame till it was perpendicular, at the same time two people held poles to the points to keep them in their proper places and prevent them slipping from the holes into which they must fit. They went in nicely and fitted exactly, and now came the nervous part to us onlookers. Two of the young men climbed up to the top and stood on the cross-beam to hammer it home with the great *beetles*. This required a steady head and active body for they were twenty feet above the under story which was full of great stones and rubbish. Charles Dunlop and John Reid were the two to go up first. Thus the six bents were put up, but when the two last were being raised heavy showers came on and interrupted the work. The other young men took it in turns to go up and beetle the mortices close. F. Haycock, F. Bray, C. Dunlop, J. Reid and E. Brown were the principal actors as being the most efficient. By the time the last bent was up it had settled into a wet evening and of course the work was stopped. So all came in except the younger boys who remained in the workshop playing marbles, etc.

We were all very merry, though the old roof let in drops in every direction and the stairs had a fine rapid stream running down them. Even the parlour was wet in several places, but all was well for the new house was advancing. The gentlemen drank the punch for which they would not delay after dinner, and those who liked smoked cigars. The young people chatted or flirted as they fancied. Miss Caddy played on the piano, and the housekeepers made preparations for tea; by this time our party had been increased by the arrival of two Miss Reids and Mr Traill. We had a large tea table; a tray and teapot at either end were presided over by Miss Haycock and Anna and there were plenty of cakes, bread and butter and strawberry jam. All went on smoothly and merrily. About half-past eight the young people said they must have some dancing. Edward Brown played the fiddle, and till eleven o'clock we passed the time between this amusement and singing. In the meantime Anna and I had laid the supper table *in the kitchen* which had been prepared for us before the servants had gone to bed. We had a cold ham at one end of the table, a pair of roast fowls at the other, the intervening space being filled with tongue, cold mutton, cakes, tarts, cups of custard and a few decanters of currant cordial (home-made). Altogether it looked very respectable, and as every one seemed determined to be pleased and happy both day and night T—— and I were much gratified . . . Next morning all were early astir and before breakfast were at work again. They placed great square logs called 'wall plates' on the bents which had been raised the day before. These plates correspond with the sills which are fixed underneath, and on the wall plates the rafters are fastened. These were in place before breakfast, afterwards nearly all our kind friends and assistants left us. F. Haycock, J. Reid and C. Dunlop stayed to help place the rafters, which was done before dinner. E. Brown has since been busy making the centre gable, he has now all the collar beams put in and is at present grooving the boards for the roof which will then be shingled. They could have done everything in one day but for the storm. But we may be thankful it was only stopped by that, for often dreadful accidents happen at these 'Raising Bees,' but T—— was careful to choose steady and experienced young men as helpers, so all was well.

FRANCES STEWART, *Our Forest Home*, 1902

I wonder if you would think our house very rough, if you were to come straight to it from the ship. What do you think the floors are covered with? A substance brought from the cattle kraal! When I first heard of it I was horrified, and declared I never would have any room of mine 'smeared,' as they call it. The floors of all our rooms are cemented, but the verandah is brick, and very soft. I was obliged to come to it at last. The way they do it is this: the girls bring the *substance* and 'flop' it down; then they pour some water on it, and go down on their knees, and spread it all over with their hands. Then the smell whilst it is being done! Ugh! They use this *substance* for almost everything. They cover the walls inside and out with it; use it like mortar; and where Mr Jackson and Mr Glover are going it will be their only fuel. When used for this last purpose it is placed in the sun to dry, and then piled away like peat. E. says he can fancy B., when reading this, bursting out laughing and saying, 'What disgusting people! only fancy E. taking that beautiful creature to live amongst such nasty ways!' No one was more decided than I was in saying that it should not be done; but we cannot afford wooden floors, and it is very difficult to get up cement. We brought four casks from Maritzburg; but it was so heavy that going up a mountain the waggon stuck, and we were obliged to take it out and leave it there, miles and miles away from a white man's house, covered with a tarpaulin. It has since been got down to the Tugela, and there it lies. So what must we do but *smear?* When it is dry, which is in about one and a half hour, it is really clean and smooth.

MRS WILKINSON, *A Lady's Life . . . in Zululand,* 1882

The success of settling in owed much to the neighbours (if there were any). Christian ones were usually *welcomed with relief.*

We live close by a large river, so I can look out of my sash-window right into the river. A very fruitful place; for apples, cherries, raspberries, grapes, plums, growing any where, *any one may get them without money,* what they please. Dear mother, I fear you will be troubled to read that side, it is put so thick; for my paper is not half big enough to say all that I want to say: but this I can say, that we want for nothing; bless God for it; for we can buy a leg of mutton every day, and green pease or French beans brought to the door, and we have got in 32 gallons of cider for 14s. I wish you was all here to help drink it. Tell my dear sister if she was here she might earn 8s. or 10s. a day; for they charge so much for work. I was forced to give 12s. for a cambric bonnet for Harriot. And now I must tell you a little what friends we met with when we landed into Hudson: *such friends as we never found in England: but it was chiefly from that people that love and fear God. We had so much meat brought us that we could not eat while it was good; a whole quarter of a calf at once; so we had 2 or 3 quarters in a little time, and 7 stone of beef. One old gentleman come and brought us a waggon load of wood, and 2 chucks of bacon. Some sent flour, some bread, some cheese, some soap, some candles, some chairs, some bedsteads. One class leader sent us 3s. worth of tin ware, and many other things; so we can truly say godliness is profitable unto all things.* We are in a land of plenty, and, above all, where we can hear the sound of the Gospel.

from WILLIAM COBBETT, *The Emigrant's Guide,* 1829

I really think Freetown is worse than England for noises at night, but they are of a very different sort; instead of carriages rolling along every minute, you have first the frogs, which commence at sunset; soon after the dogs begin to bark, and never cease till midnight; at different times you hear the monkeys chattering, donkeys braying, and the crown birds screeching; and at dawn you might fancy yourself surrounded by poultry yards, there is such a crowing and cackling . . . There is another sound at five o'clock in the morning, which, although it wakes one rather earlier than usual, is very grateful when you remember the people you are among, and how different they would be, were it not for the blessed efforts of the Missionaries; I mean: the singing in the Chapels.

[MARY CHURCH], *Sierra Leone*, 1835

[N]ight at the diggings is the characteristic time: murder here—murder there—revolvers cracking—blunderbusses bombing—rifles going off—balls whistling—one man groaning with a broken leg—another shouting because he couldn't find the way to his hole, and a third equally vociferous because he has tumbled into one—this man swearing—another praying—a party of bacchanals chanting various ditties to different time and tune, or rather minus both. Here is one man grumbling because he has brought his wife with him, another ditto because he has left his behind, or sold her for an ounce of gold or a bottle of rum. Donny-brook Fair is not to be compared to an evening at Bendigo . . .

In some tents the soft influence of our sex is pleasingly apparent: the tins are as bright as silver, there are sheets as well as blankets on the beds, and perhaps a clean counterpane, with the addition of a dry sack or piece of carpet on the ground; whilst a pet cockatoo, chained to a perch, makes noise enough to keep the 'missus' from feeling lonely when the good man is at work. Sometimes a wife is at first rather a nuisance; women get scared and frightened, then cross, and commence a 'blow up' with their husbands; but all their railing generally ends in their quietly settling down to this rough and primitive style of living, if not without a murmur, at least to all appearance with the determination to laugh and bear it. And although rough in their manners, and not over select in their address, the digger seldom wilfully injures a woman . . .

The stores at the diggings are large tents generally square or oblong, and everything required by a digger can be obtained for money, from sugar-candy to potted anchovies; from East India pickles to Bass's pale ale; from ankle jack boots to a pair of stays; from a baby's cap to a cradle; and every apparatus for mining, from a pick to a needle. But the confusion—the din—the medley—what a scene for a shop walker! Here lies a pair of herrings dripping into a bag of sugar, or a box of raisins; there a gay-looking bundle of ribbons beneath two tumblers, and a half-finished bottle of ale. Cheese and butter, bread and yellow soap, pork and currants, saddles and frocks, wide-awakes and blue serge shirts, green veils and shovels, baby linen and tallow candles, are all heaped indiscriminately together; added to which, there are children bawling, men swearing, store-keeper sulky, and last, not *least*, women's tongues going nineteen to the dozen.

ELLEN CLACY, *A Lady's Visit to the Gold Diggings*, 1853

We like our station better and better; it is far pleasanter than Madras, which was like England in a perspiration . . .

[JULIA MAITLAND], *Letters from Madras . . . By a Lady*, 1843

The climate—so beloved a subject in emigrant diaries and letters home—was rarely less than an inconvenience, and frequently far more.

I am sorry to find that you see so many alarming paragraphs in the newspapers about the deadliness of this climate: that it is not at all suited to European constitutions it would be worse than folly to deny; still, owing to the cutting down of trees, the clearing of 'bush' with more general cultivation, the colony is much more healthy than it used to be. One great method of preserving health is to banish all anxiety on the subject: therefore at the same time that I scrupulously obey every injunction to avoid all over-fatigue, exposure to the sun, land-wind, damp and draughts, I can truly say I do not fear for myself.

ELIZABETH MELVILLE, *A Residence at Sierra Leone*, 1849

March 4, 1794. Though I wore 3 fur tippets I was so cold I could hardly hold my Cards this evening. This is the first time we have felt the want of a ceiling which we have not made in our drawing Room because the Room was rather low . . .

ELIZABETH SIMCOE, *Diary . . . of Upper Canada, 1792–6*, ed. J. Ross Robertson, 1911

During this very cold weather I was surprised by the frequent recurrence of a phenomenon that I suppose was of an electrical nature. When the frosts were most intense I noticed that when I undressed, my clothes, which are at this cold season chiefly of woollen cloth, or lined with flannel, gave out when moved a succession of sounds, like the crackling and snapping of a fire, and in the absence of a candle emitted sparks of a pale whitish blue light, similar to the flashes produced by cutting loaf-sugar in the dark, or stroking the back of a black cat.

CATHERINE TRAILL, *The Backwoods of Canada*, 1836

[*Tuesday 10 January 1792*] I bought an Eiderdown quilt which cost £4 16s.

12th. I drove out in a covered Carriole.

18th. A Ball at the Chateau, this being Queen Charlotte's birth-night, there were near 300 people. The ladies were well dressed.

21st. Miss Johnson dined with me, & we went to a dance in the Evening at the Fusiliers' Mess Room—very agreeable. The Thermometer 24 degrees below . . .

24th. I gave a dance & supper to a dozen of the Fusiliers & as many young dancing Ladies. My Rooms being so small obliged me to invite so few & only those who danced.

29th. Drove in a covered Carriole towards the Isle of Orleans: the Ice was so rough & snow uneven that I was almost seasick . . .

31st. A very pleasant dance at the Chateau this evening.

[*Tuesday 7 February*] At two o'clock the kitchen chimney was on fire. It was soon extinguished as the people here are expert in using fire engines . . . Prince Edward, General Clarke etc., dined with Coll. Simcoe & this accident retarded the dinner, so I went to bed before the dinner.

ELIZABETH SIMCOE, *Diary . . . of Upper Canada, 1792–6*,
ed. J. Ross Robertson, 1911

But the dinner went on. And the dances and the soirées and the rest. No matter where any British oasis might be, as long as it was settled by the right sort of people, there was no reason at all why life should not go on (with only the scantest regard to the unlovely natives and elements) just as it had in the drawing rooms of home.

Besides the bazaar the station contains the Court House, the District Bungalow, and the Post Office; half-a-dozen European houses scattered up and down the clearing, and the club.

To the Anglo-Indians the club seems as necessary to existence as the air they breathe. I verily believe that when the white man penetrates into the interior to found a colony, his first act is to clear a space and build a club house.

The Club House at Remyo is a truly imposing looking edifice, perched high on the hill side, standing in a well kept compound, surrounded by its offices, bungalows, and stables. About the interior of the building I must confess ignorance, it being an unpardonable offence for any woman to cross the threshold. It may be that it is but a whited sepulchre, the exterior beautiful beyond description, the interior merely emptiness: I cannot tell.

At the foot of the Club House stands a tiny one-roomed mat hut, the most unpretentious building I ever beheld, universally known by the imposing title of 'The Ladies Club.' Here two or more ladies of the station nightly assemble for an hour before dinner, to read the two months old magazines, to search vainly through the shelves of the 'library' for a book they have not read more than three times, to discuss the iniquities of the native cook, and to pass votes of censure on the male sex for condemning them to such an insignificant building.

It has always been a sore point with the ladies of Remyo that their Club House only contains one room. They argue that if half the members wish to play whist, and the other half wished to talk, many inconveniences (to say the least) would arise. As there are but four lady members of the club this argument does not appear to me to be convincing, but I do not pretend to understand the intricacies of club life.

BETH ELLIS, *An English Girl's First Impressions of Burmah*, 1899

Jim is distinctly 'given to hospitality', and has a special aptitude for discovering the maimed, the halt, and the blind, and inviting them to a feast. He even suffers bores gladly.

ANNE WILSON, *Letters from India*, 1911

Never shall I forget that first official luncheon. How strange and forlorn I felt and how I longed for someone who would stick up for me!

When luncheon was over we three ladies left the men downstairs and established ourselves upstairs in the drawing-room. Mrs Crookshank and Mrs Helms then proceeded to discuss the new Bishop Chambers and his wife. 'Horrid woman!' said Mrs Crookshank. 'She will want to go in to dinner before me. However,' she continued in a serene but very decided voice, 'my husband is the Rajah's prime minister, and prime ministers' wives always take precedence over bishops' wives.' Then, turning to me, she said with rather a forced smile, 'And what are *you* to be called? I hear that Mrs Chambers has put it about that it would be wrong to call you "Ranee." ' 'Why?' I said.

'Because, dear, you would not like people to imagine that you were a *black* woman!' 'But Sarawak people are *not* black,' said I, remembering the four dear Datus, their courtesy and politeness on being presented to me. 'I should rather *like* being taken for a Malay.' 'Well!!!' exclaimed both the ladies. And there, for the time, the matter rested.

LADY MARGARET BROOKE, *Good Morning and Good Night,*
1934

We do not, in general, encourage [the natives] to come to our houses, as you may conceive there are some offensive circumstances, which makes their company by no means desirable unless it be those who live wholly with us. A good deal of their language (if it may so be called) is now understood but we can learn nothing from them.

ELIZABETH MACARTHUR, *Journal,* [1791]

A day of much trial and vexation, the Native boys so very insulting, I could not bear it. We leave all that is dear to us on earth for their sake and they do all they can to irritate and make us angry . . .

ELIZA WHITE in Frances Porter's and Charlotte MacDonald's
My Hand Will Write What My Heart Dictates, 1996

Perhaps 'God's police', those good and virtuous women intro-duced at the beginning of this anthology, were not always as welcome amongst the indigenous populations of the Empire as they might fancy.

Robertson brought his bit of Brown wt. him to the settlement this spring in the hopes that she would pick up a few English manners before visiting the civilized World . . . I told him distinctly that the thing was impossible, which mortified him exceedingly.

FRANCES SIMPSON, *Diary,* 1833

I came to Nome in the late spring of 1900, a New York stenographer lured by tales of Alaskan gold. Coincidence, circumstance and plain luck had brought me there, armed with only my typewriter. And several years passed before I could decide whether that luck had been good or bad. There were times when it looked very bad indeed.

Until January of that year, I had been working in the office of the Hope Mining Company at Basin, Montana. I was the stenographer and bookkeeper, and had little contact with the actual operations of quartz mining. But I determined to learn as much as possible of the work, and presented myself at the entrance of the shaft.

'No women in here,' said a miner.

'Why not? I work in the office.'

'Makes no difference if you own the office, Miss Fitz. Women aren't allowed in this shaft. Bad luck.'

Later, the mine superintendent explained. Superstition held that disaster would soon follow a woman's visit to a mine. And, silly as the belief was, it effectively kept me from learning much of anything of quartz mining.

A short time after this, two women applied for permission to visit the mine. They were refused, but somehow managed to sneak into the shaft. Soon after they left, fire broke out in the timbering, trapping some of the workers underground. Seven miners died in the flames—seven men whose lives, the survivors swore, had been sacrificed because two women dared flout an old and valid belief.

FRANCES ELLA FITZ, *Lady Sourdough*, 1951

I must not forget to tell the story of my dear child Nietfong, although it is a very sad one. She was the daughter of the Chinese baker who lived in the lane which led from our garden to the town. I used to befriend her mother, a delicate little woman, very roughly treated by her husband. She twice ran to me for shelter when her husband beat her, and though of course I always had to give her up to him when he came begging for her the next day, he knew what I thought of him, and had a sort of respect for me in consequence.

This poor woman died young, and left one little girl about four years old. Nietfong used to come up to day-school when she was old enough, and in 1858, when I was so happy as to have an English governess for my Mab, I took the little Chinese girl to live with us and join Mab in her lessons. She was quite a little lady, so gentle, teachable, and well mannered. In 1860 we took our children to England . . .

We returned in 1861, leaving three children in England, and brought a baby girl out with us. As I walked up the lane to the mission-house, Nietfong stood watching for me at the gate. 'Take me home with you; oh, I am so glad you are come back!' So I took her home, and Nietfong told me that her father had married and that her step-mother was unkind to her, and beat her when she said the prayers I had taught her night and morning; 'but,' said the child, 'I always prayed, nevertheless.' She lived with us till she was about thirteen, perhaps not so much; then her father came to the Bishop and said he had sold Nietfong for a good sum of money to a man in China, and must send her there to stay with her grandmother.

In vain I entreated Acheck not to be so wicked. 'Tell me how much you would get for your daughter,' I said, 'and we will give you the money.' He laughed, and said I could not afford it, mentioning a large sum, but I do not remember what it was; so I had to break the sad news to Nietfong . . .

We shall not know the sequel of her history until by God's mercy we meet her in the heavenly home.

HARRIETTE MCDOUGALL, *Sketches of Our Life at Sarawak*,
[1882]

I told him I would not go to a church where the people who worked for us were parted off from us as if they had the pest, and we should catch it of them. I asked him, for I was curious to know, how they managed to administer the sacrament to a mixed congregation? He replied, oh, very easily; that the white portion of the assembly received it first, and the blacks afterward. *A new commandment I give unto you, that ye love one another, even as I have loved you.* Oh, what a shocking mockery! However, they show their faith, at all events, in the declaration that God is no respecter of persons, since they do not pretend to exclude from His table those whom they most certainly would not admit to their own . . . Oh, if you could imagine how this title 'Missis', addressed to me and to my children, shocks all my feelings! Several times I have exclaimed: 'For God's sake do not call me that!' and only been awakened, by the stupid amazement of the poor creatures I was addressing, to the perfect uselessness of my thus expostulating with them; once or twice, indeed, I have done more—I have explained to them and they appeared to comprehend me well, that I had no ownership over them, for that I held such ownership sinful, and that, though I was the wife of a man who pretends to own them, I was, in truth, no more their mistress than they were mine. Some of them, I know, understood me; more of them did not.

FRANCES BUTLER [KEMBLE], *Journal*, 1835

The Indian tribes on Canadian territory are Blackfeet and Piegans. The former used to number over ten thousand, but now are comparatively few. The small-pox, which raged among them in 1870, decimated their numbers; also alcohol, first introduced by Americans who established themselves on Belly River, about 1866, and in which they drove a roaring trade, as the Indians sacrificed everything for this 'fire-water,' as they called it, and hundreds died in consequence of exposure and famine, having neither clothes to cover them nor horses nor weapons wherewith to hunt. Luckily in 1874 the mounted police put an entire end to this abominable sale of whisky.

MRS CECIL HALL, *A Lady's Life on a Farm in Manitoba*, 1884

How different would be the state of almost everything in this Colony, were that greatest curse man ever created out of God's good gifts, intoxicating liquor, less easily obtained by those who *ought* to be the industrious and prosperous, but, alas! too generally *are* the idle and worthless part of the community. Time, money, character, decency, feeling, principle, ambition, and honesty—all are sacrificed to the demoralizing passion for rum, when once it gains the ascendency; and to know how often that is, we need only observe and listen to the sad evidence so continually passing around us. I perhaps praise the tidy appearance and good cookery of a friend's servant: 'Ah! yes, she is an excellent cook, but we can so seldom keep her *sober*.' The coachman of another seems quite a model for his class, till you hear he is so confirmed a drunkard that his mistress dares not trust him to drive her home alone from a party. Another family have an honest old 'major-domo,' faithful and good in every other point; may be trusted with 'untold gold,' but not with a bottle of rum. It is a universal failing, and a really sober servant or mechanic may consequently be held as a pearl of great price. Age and sex make no difference; your dainty lady's-maid or pretty young nurse-girl is just as likely to be over-liberal in her libations to Bacchus as your groom or shoeblack; and no threats, no bribes, no punishments avail to keep the besotted creatures from the dram-bottle, if it be by any means or in any shape accessible. I have known a female servant drink camphorated spirits of wine, and suspect the same individual of consuming a pint of hartshorn which mysteriously disappeared about the same time from my room; its evident strength being no doubt too tempting. Eau de Cologne and lavender-water, I know, they drink whenever they are left about, or anything else believed to contain spirit. The universality of this vice is most dreadful to contemplate, and far worse to witness and endure.

CATHERINE TRAILL, *The Canadian Settler's Guide*, 1860

FIVE

SPENDING THE DAY

*On Thursday morning early we were up preparing for a long day's
journey. Though only about 25 miles distant, ten hours is the time
required to reach Antong. Ten hours . . . by wheelbarrow. Oh,
inexpressible experience!*
Geraldine Guinness, *In the Far East*, [1889]

Miss Guinness was a missionary. She was expected to
weather inexpressible experiences in the course of her
duty: ten hours by wheelbarrow was all in a day's work. Mind
you, other missionaries in this chapter did not have it quite so
hard: Keturah Jeffreys was carried about Madagascar in a kind
of cot (admittedly with her head somewhat lower than her feet
for half the time), while Jane Moir relished being on the move
in Tanzania for miles and days at a time—on foot.

Travel was one way of spending the day, if the necessity or
opportunity arose. For lay women it was usually a question of
making or returning visits, or gathering material, perhaps, for a
book. And curiosity, of course. But there were plenty of other
pastimes, depending on who and where one was. The upper eche-
lons of British Indian society, for instance, enjoyed days stuffed
with 'calls', club activities, interminable dinner parties, and all
the engrossing observances of etiquette and custom. Gardening
was popular with those for whom working on the land was an
option rather than an obligation; the study of natural history
was a delightful occupation, too, as were (for the lustier) riding,
fishing, and big-game hunting.

All these pursuits helped animate the leaden background of
boredom so many of the more privileged emigrant women

seemed to dread. For, this chapter has little to do with the home-
steaders, the frontierswomen, and those fighting every day to
keep their heads above water and their families alive: boredom
was a luxury they could ill afford. It is more about emigrant
ladies *than women. And, in the following case, literally so:*

There happened a great *contre temps* this afternoon. I was to be at
home to receive visitors; so Lady Harriet and I sat in state, and
nobody came! At five D. returned home, and I said to him, 'Not a
single soul has come to see us.' Tea came in, and he asked, 'Has
nobody called?' 'Oh, yes,' said the servant, 'but I said, "Not at
home."' We sent for the book, and found 104 people had been, so we
had to sit down and write 104 notes to explain. I had a dinner party
in the evening, and, luckily, no-one seems to have been offended.

LADY HARRIOT DUFFERIN, *My Canadian Journal*, 1891

The parties in Bombay are the most dull and uncomfortable meetings one can imagine. Forty or fifty persons assemble at seven
o'clock, and stare at one another till dinner is announced, when the
ladies are handed to table, according to the strictest rules of prece-
dency, by a gentleman of a rank corresponding to their own. At
table there can be no general conversation, but the different
couples who have been paired off, and who, on account of their
rank, invariably sit together at every great dinner, amuse themselves with remarks on the company, as satirical as their wit will
allow; and woe be to the stranger, whose ears are certain of being
regaled with the catalogue of his supposed imperfections and
misfortunes, and who has the chance of learning more of his own
history than in all probability he ever knew before. After dinner the
same topics continue to occupy the ladies, with the addition of lace,
jewels, intrigues, and the latest fashions; or if there be any newly-
arrived young women, the making or breaking of matches for them
furnish employment for the ladies of the colony till the arrival of
the next cargo. Such is the company at an English Bombay feast.
    The repast itself is as costly as possible, and in such profusion
that no part of the table-cloth remains uncovered. But the dinner

is scarcely touched, as every person eats a hearty meal called tiffin at two o'clock, at home. Each guest brings his own servant, sometimes two or three; these are either Parsees or Mussulmans [Moslems]. It appears singular to a stranger to see behind every white man's chair a dark, long-bearded, turbaned gentleman, who usually stands so close to his master, as to make no trifling addition to the heat of the apartment; indeed, were it not for the *punka* . . . which is suspended over every table and kept constantly swinging, in order to freshen the air, it would scarcely be possible to sit out the melancholy ceremony of an Indian dinner.

MARIA GRAHAM, *Letters on India*, 1814

The dinner party is the most general form of entertainment in Remyo, but not of very frequent occurrence; the reasons being, the limited number of available guests and the restricted nature of the menu. No sane person would dream of inviting another sane person to dine upon nothing but Burmese chicken, even displayed in various disguises from soup to savoury.

Once a week beef can be obtained, so dinner parties are usually given on 'beef days.' Should an invitation arrive for another date great excitement prevails as to what special delicacy has been procured.

Once we were presented with a peacock, and gave a dinner party to celebrate the event, the peacock itself being the chief item of the celebration. Our guests arrived full of anticipation of some unknown treat, we received them 'big with pride.'

But alas! the vanity of human hopes. During the early part of the dinner, over the chicken entrées, the conversation turned upon the relative merits as food of various kinds of fowl. One of our guests, a man full to overflowing with information on every subject interesting and otherwise suddenly announced cheerfully:

'One bird I may tell you is not fit for human food, and that bird is a peacock.'

Thereupon ensued an awful pause, in the midst of which the servants entered, carrying the peacock in all its glory.

BETH ELLIS, *An English Girl's First Impressions of Burmah*, 1899

One of the saving graces of life in a British station is the unvarying observance of the small conventions which mark the society of civilization. A man may be the only European official, with no neighbour nearer than one hundred miles, but he or his wife (if he has one) will dress as carefully for their lonely dinner as if in the midst of a London Season, and the gleaming candles, the flowers and quiet, unobtrusive service are considered as essential in Africa as in Mayfair or Upper Fifth Avenue.

ANNE DUNDAS, *Beneath African Glaciers*, 1924

I fully realised during this summer, that solitude in the Bush is not privacy. Though in case of any accident I was out of reach of all human help, yet I was liable at any moment of the day to have some passing settler walk coolly in, and sit down in my very chair if I had vacated it for a moment. I got one fright which I shall not easily forget. I had given your two brothers their breakfast, and they had started for their hay-making in the distant beaver meadow. I had washed up the breakfast-things, cleared everything away, and was arranging my hair in the glass hanging in the bed-place, the curtain of which was undrawn on account of the heat. My parting look in the glass disclosed a not very prepossessing face in the doorway behind, belonging to a man who stood there immovable as a statue, and evidently enjoying my discomfiture.

I greeted him with a scream, which was almost a yell, and advanced pale as a ghost, having the agreeable sensation of all the blood in my body running down to my toes! His salutation was:

'Wall, I guess I've skeered you some!'

'Yes!' I replied, 'you startled me very much.'

He then came in and sat down. I sat down too, and we fell into quite an easy flow of talk about the weather, the crops, etc.

How devoutly I wished him anywhere else, and how ill I felt after my fright, I need not say, but I flatter myself that nothing of this appeared on the surface; all was courtesy and politeness.

At length he went way, and finding your brother in the beaver meadow, took care to inform him that he 'had had quite a pleasant chat with his old woman!'

[HARRIET KING], Letters from Muskoka By An Emigrant Lady, 1878

I really believe the Madras ladies spend all their time in writing notes—'chits,'—as they are called. I do not know ten people now, and yet there never passes a day without my having one or two 'chits' to answer:—what with writing them, composing them, finding my penknife, mending my pen, hunting for proper note-paper, which is always hidden in some scribbled foolscap beginnings of tracts, or such-like, all my morning is hindered;—and, their chits are generally only to say how sorry they are they have not been able to call lately, that I must have wondered at it, and *thought* . . . Now, I never *think* . . . and I would always rather they did not call, because I must sit all day with my hair dressed and my best clothes on, waiting for them:—remember the thermometer is at 92°.

[JULIA MAITLAND], Letters from Madras . . . By a Lady, 1843

One crying fault of the 'ladies' prevails far more in colonial than in English society—I allude to that most absurd fallacy, which seems to imagine that a lady ought to be discovered by any chance visitor, at any hour of the day, fully arrayed in her newest attire, and in a state of smartness and precision, as regards flounces, ribbons, and collars, which is wholly and utterly incompatible with any kind of domestic occupation or duty whatsoever.

Now the prevalence of this monstrous belief is productive of many evils; not the least of which is, the delay which almost invariably takes place in the appearance of the ladies of any family on whom one calls in the country; and the period allotted for a friendly chat thus passes in a dreary survey of a formal drawing-room, or in constrained talk with the unhappy master of the house, who is in a fidget of anxiety and impatience at the absence of wife and daughters. Thus, unless we determine to let our own dinner spoil, or to omit some other intended visit, we are compelled to take leave in five minutes after the entrance of our fair friends, whose recently-smoothed hair, horizontally-folded dresses, and red damp hands, attest with painful certainty the trouble which our kindly-intended call has occasioned them.

I know I am on dangerous ground, and that I might almost as safely 'patter in a hornet's nest,' as show myself so manifestly a traitor in the camp; yet a little exposure of such follies ofttimes effects so much improvement, that I do not hesitate to take my share of responsibility in the attempt. The golden rule by which all such troublesome transformations may be rendered unnecessary is, of course, to avoid ever being untidy or slatternly, let our occupation be what it may.

My own criterion of propriety in every-day dress is a very simple one. Of all persons living, I consider my husband to merit my first and chiefest respect; and if my attire is such as I deem neat and proper to be worn in *his* presence, I do not think I ought to suppose it unfit to appear in before indifferent people or strangers. And it seems to me far more pleasant to imagine one's lady-friends notably busy in a morning, as good country housewives must be and are, than to conceive such useless impossibilities as ladies (some of whom in this place, I know, keep no female servant) dressed in new silks or muslins at noon, and seated on a sofa, doing nothing!

LOUISA MEREDITH, My Home in Tasmania, 1852

Quite. Some good sense did prevail, then (despite the evidence of these last few extracts), amongst those ladies lucky enough to have the odd hour or two at their disposal.

Thursday, July 18 [1839]. This morning, after sundry deliberations concerning the wind, and whether the southerly direction was likely to bring rain soon or not, it was determined that John and I should set out to carry our invitation to the Dunsfords.

Accordingly I embarked for the first time on board the *Ninniwish*, and a very nice little boat it is, but I rather prefer a canoe for an expedition of moderate length. I don't know how I should bear the kneeling position for three or four hours in a canoe. I can take a paddle, and at least flatter myself that I do some little good, which is more agreeable than sitting in state at one end of the boat, and having nothing to do but observe my companion's exertions. But my canoeing days are over. John does not like the responsibility of taking me out in one, and thinks it altogether an unfit conveyance for so helpless a being as woman. I, having a due value for my precious life, should be sorry to urge the risk of it, but I am rather glad the idea did not spring up earlier. After we turned Sturgeon Point the wind was favourable. We put up a small sail, and proceeded more swiftly and easily on our voyage. It was the first time that I had been lower down than the Point since we came up—now almost two years ago. I think the lower part of the lake, upon the whole, superior to our end in point of beauty. Both shores are pretty, and the islands make an agreeable variety. Though at our end our own side is inferior to no part of the lake, the opposite coast is very monotonous. Mr Dunsford's new house is a conspicuous object all the way down, and, I daresay itself commands a fine view, but it will be two or three months more, I fancy, before they will be able to get into it. We found the ladies luxuriating in the absence of all domestics, a variety of not unfrequent enjoyment in the backwoods. Their servant had taken her departure early one morning before the family were up, and since that the young ladies were taking it in turn to bake bread, make puddings, etc., and perform all the labours of the household. We can speak for the skill they have acquired in the first-named operation, for nicer bread was never laid on Canadian table than they placed before us, not even my own! After we had done justice to it, Mrs Dunsford provided a further entertainment of harp and piano to enliven us during a thunderstorm. Our invitation was not accepted, which on some accounts I did not regret. We afterwards crossed the lake to Mr Fraser's. He was absent, but we found his nice little wife at home and gave them the invitation just declined by the Dunsfords, which was conditionally accepted. Here, I saw and smelled the first roses since I came to Canada. Their little cottage is very pretty, with the wild vine and roses round the pillars of the verandah, and something more like a garden in front of it than can be elsewhere seen in these parts. We spent an hour or two very pleasantly with Mrs Fraser. She is a very pleasing, unaffected person, and when we departed I wished she was nearer to us. Four hours' pulling against adverse wind brought us to our own landing just about sunset, and all the familiar objects about my home seemed to greet me with the same sort of old acquaintanceship as formerly after a long journey and an absence of weeks.

ANN LANGTON, *A Gentlewoman in Upper Canada*,
ed. H. H. Langton 1950

In general . . . I rise at five o'Clock in the morning, read till Seven, then take a walk in the garden or field, see that the Servants are at their respective business, then to breakfast. The first hour after breakfast is spent at my musick, the next is constantly employed in recollecting something I have learned lest for want of practise it should be quite lost, such as French and short hand. After that I devote the rest of the time till I dress for dinner to our little Polly and two black girls who I teach to read, and if I have my paps's approbation (my Mamas I have got) I intend [them] for school mistres's for the rest of the Negroe children—another scheme you see. But to proceed, the first hour after dinner as the first after breakfast at musick, the rest of the afternoon in Needle work till candle light, and from that time to bed time read or write. 'Tis the fashion here to carry our work abroad with us so that having company, without they are great strangers, is no interruption to that affair; but I have particular matters for particular days, which is an interruption to mine. Mondays my musick Master is here. Tuesdays my friend Mrs Chardon (about 3 mile distant) and I are constantly engaged to each other, she at our house one Tuesday—I at hers the next and this is one of the happiest days I spend at Woppoe. Thursday the whole day except what the necessary affairs of the family take up is spent in writing, either on the business of the plantations, or letters to my friends. Every other Fryday, if no company, we go a vizeting so that I go abroad once a week and no oftener.

Now you may form some judgment what time I can have to work my lappets. I own I never go to them with a quite easey conscience as I know my father has an aversion to my employing my time in that poreing work, but they are begun and must be finished. I hate to undertake any thing and not go thro' with it; but by way of relaxation from the other I have begun a peice of work of a quicker sort which requires nither Eyes nor genius—at least not very good ones. Would you ever guess it to be a shrimp nett? For so it is.

O! I had like to forgot the last thing I have done a great while. I have planted a large figg orchard with design to dry and export them. I have reckoned my expence and the prophets to arise from these figgs, but was I to tell you how great an Estate I am to make this way, and how 'tis to be laid out you would think me far gone in romance. Your good Uncle I know has long thought I have a fertile brain at schemeing. I only confirm him in his opinion; but I own I love the vegitable world extremly. I think it an innocent and useful amusement.

ELIZA LUCAS PINCKNEY, *The Letterbook 1739–1762*,
ed. Elise Pinckney, 1972

And an amusement shared—given the dearth of other 'innocent and useful' ones—by many.

There are certain customs which the native gardeners observe, to which, from my own experience, I would advise a newcomer to pay attention, at any rate until he can prove to his own satisfaction that they are mere fallacy. For instance, they say that a vine must only be pruned two days before the full moon, and rose trees when the moon is young. Again, they say that root vegetables such as potatoes, onions, Jerusalem artichokes, etc., should be planted when the nights are dark, and those which bear above ground, such as melons, peas, beans, tomatoes, etc., just before or after full moon, when the nights are light.

KATHERINE BURDON, *A Handbook of St Kitts*, 1920

I walked this Evening in a wood lately set on fire by some unextinguished fires being left by some persons who had encamped there, which in dry weather often communicates to the trees. Perhaps you have no idea of the pleasure of walking in a burning wood, but I found it so great that I think I shall have some woods set on fire for my evening walks. The smoke arising from it keeps the mosquitoes at a distance & where the fire has caught the hollow trunk of a lofty tree the flame issuing from the top has a fine effect. In some trees where but a small flame appears it looks like stars as the Evening grows dark, & the flare & smoke, interspersed in different masses of dark woods, has a very picturesque appearance a little like Tasso's 'enchanted wood.'

The author came to a settler's cottage, home of a Mr Green and his family.

They prepared me some refreshment at this House; some excellent Cakes baked on the coals; Eggs; a boiled black squirrel; tea & Coffee made of Peas which was good . . .

The Sugar was made from black Walnut Trees, which looks darker than that from the Maple, but I think it is sweeter.

Green's wife died a year ago & left ten Children who live here with their father in a House consisting of a Room, a Closet & a loft, but being New Jersey people their House is delicately clean & neat, & not the appearance of being inhabited by 3 people, every part is so neatly kept. I sent a Boy to gather a flower I forgot to bring from the Mountain & he met a Rattle Snake. We rode back to the 'King's Head' to dinner.

ELIZABETH SIMCOE, *The Diary* . . . *1792–6*,
ed. J. Ross Robertson, 1911

I kept a collection of insects, such as moths, butterflies, and dragonflies, some of which are very beautiful to look at, but if intended to be copied they must be carefully smoked to death, or they will very soon lose their beauty. [T]his cruel little job is done by quickly putting a tumbler over the creature, under which you slip a piece

of paper and then light as many matches as will fill the tumbler
with smoke: the poor thing then is soon dead, and in a few days
there is nothing but its shell to be seen, and when put in the sun,
and properly dried, it is fit to be put up in pepper (black pepper is
the best to use), which will preserve them for three or four years.

ELIZABETH COLLINS, *Memories of the Southern States*, 1865

*Other and more vigorous pastimes were available to livelier
ladies of leisure.*

As the result of my own experience, I *most* strongly advise every
woman who intends to do much riding out here, especially in the
way of marching, to abandon her side-saddle altogether, and adopt
the 'astride' position. In the first place, it is far more comfortable
and less tiring on a long march; secondly, it does away with the
necessity of bringing out special saddlery for oneself, it makes one
quite independent of being 'put up,' and also enables one to march
in the most comfortable of clothes, a short divided skirt or
bloomers, putties and shooting boots; thirdly, and most important
of all, it is the greatest blessing to the pony. No matter how straight
you sit, sooner or later the strain of a side-saddle begins to tell on
a pony, from the mere fact that the weight of the rider's two legs is
on one side of him! I noticed this especially at Katāgum when
riding horses which had never carried a side-saddle before, and so
sensitive were they to the innovation that it was almost impossible
to keep them in the road at all—they bored so badly to the near
side.

CONSTANCE LARYMORE, *A Resident's Wife in Nigeria*, 1908

Having made a fresh, and, as I thought, promising purchase of fishing tackle, Jack and I betook ourselves to the river, and succeeded in
securing some immense catfish, of which, to tell you the truth, I am
most horribly afraid when I have caught them. The dexterity necessary for taking them off the hook so as to avoid the spikes on their

backs, and the spikes on each side of their gills, the former having to be pressed down, and the two others pressed up, before you can get any purchase on the slimy beast (for it is smooth skinned and without scales, to add to the difficulty)—these conditions, I say, make the catching of catfish questionable sport. Then, too, they hiss, and spit, and swear at one, and are altogether devilish in their aspect and demeanor: nor are they good for food, except, as Jack with much humility said this morning, for colored folks: 'Good for colored folks, missis; me 'spect not good enough for white people.'

FRANCES KEMBLE, *Journal*, 1863

I come now to speak of a delusion which is very general in the 'old country,' and in which I largely shared. I mean with regard to the great abundance of venison and game to be found in these parts. This fallacy is much encouraged by different books on emigration, which speak of these desirable articles of food as being plentiful, and within the reach of every settler.

I certainly arrived with a vague notion that passing deer might be shot from one's own door, that partridge and wild-duck were as plentiful as sparrows in England, and that hares and rabbits might almost be caught with the hand. These romantic ideas were ruefully dispelled! There is little game of any kind left, and to get that good dogs are wanted, which are very expensive to keep.

None of our party have caught the most distant glimpse of a deer since we came, except your two brothers, who once saw a poor dog rush madly across the corner of C——s' clearing, hotly pursued by a trapper's deer-hound, at a season when it was against the law to shoot deer. Your sister-in-law once, venturing from C——s' clearing to ours without an escort, was much alarmed at hearing a rustling in the 'Bush' quite near her, and a repeated 'Ba—a, ba—a!' We were told that the noise must have come from an ancient stag which is said to have haunted for years the range of rock near us. This mythical old fellow has, however, never been seen, even by the 'oldest inhabitant.'

[HARRIET KING], *Letters from Muskoka By An Emigrant Lady*, 1878

79

Don't forget to take [on camp] the indispensible mincing-machine; if necessary at headquarters, it is doubly so in the bush, where you frequently have to eat meat an hour or so after it has been killed.

CONSTANCE LARYMORE, *A Resident's Wife in Nigeria*, 1908

On the tiny South Atlantic island of Tristan da Cunha, any diversion was welcome. A ship heaving over the horizon afforded enough excitement to last perhaps half a year.

Tuesday, July 10.—An eventful day—the one we have been look-ing for. When I was resting after lunch there came a quick tap at the back door, and William hurried in to say a ship was in sight. We all rushed out, and getting on to higher ground saw her sails. We could also see our men running home from their work. We stood at Bill Rogers' gate where others had collected. They soon scattered to get ready to put off, though the wind was high and the sea rough. Children were sent out to catch the animals for barter. We came back to get our letters ready; among them were orders for groceries to the Army and Navy stores and to Messrs Cartwright's at Cape Town. Mrs Swain, junior, came in for our letters and told us only four men were going, her husband, Tom and Bill Rogers and Henry Green. We went down with her to the shore and met Ben who had come to fetch our letters as the boat was ready to start. We saw them hoist their sail and watched on with Mrs Martha Green, Betty and Repetto until it began to grow dusk.

Mrs Bob Green had tea with us, and a little later Repetto came in anxious to have a talk. He and Graham stood at the front door trying in vain to make out the ship. Soon others came in to ask for oil and candle for their lanterns, so that they might be ready to meet the returning boat. At about six o'clock we turned out and made for the fire which had been lighted on the cliff. We had some difficulty in crossing the stream as we had no lantern. Looking after the fire was Rebekah, and later there came Mrs Green, Alfred, Bob Green and the two other wives. The wind was blowing cold, and we were glad to sit near the blaze. You can picture the scene; pitchy darkness all round except where now and again gleams of light fell on the sounding sea below and made dimly visible the white line of surf. After staying some time, as there was no sign of the boat, we and the women went home.

It is now nine o'clock and still no sign of the men.

Wednesday, July 11.—As we were getting up news came that the boat was returning. We went down to the beach and found every one there and the boat just coming in. It had reached the vessel, which was bound for Australia. Henry Green went on board, and the captain, who seemed a very kind man, was able to let them have a barrel of flour, biscuits, and other things, and would have spared more had there been time . . . As regards the stores obtained, only those who went out to the ship and the widows will share in them. The rule is a man must go himself, unless ill or absent, to have a share in anything obtained in the name of the community. Sheep, geese, fowls, eggs and potatoes are the things bartered. It has been very difficult to settle down to-day.

K. M. BARROW, *Three Years in Tristan da Cunha*, 1910

Elsewhere, the boredom was all-enveloping, and even dangerous.

The irksome monotony of my daily life had produced a most unpleasant feeling in my mind. Not only had I lost much of my wonted energy, but a kind of lethargy seemed to have crept over me; a most undefinable reluctance to move about had imperceptibly gained ascendancy over my actions;—to walk, to speak (and here I must not forget to mention that my voice had become extremely feeble)—to apply myself to drawing, reading, or, in fact, to make the slightest exertion of any kind whatever, had become absolutely irksome to me.

It was not the feeling of what we Europeans call *ennui* which I experienced, for that sensation can always be shook off by a little moral courage and energy; but it was a state bordering on that frightful melancholy, that must, if not dispelled, engender insanity.

EMILY LOTT, *The English Governess in Egypt*, 1866

In conversation with my daughter-in-law, who was often unavoidably alone for the whole day, we mutually agreed that there were times when the sense of loneliness became so dreadful, that had a bear jumped in at the window, or the house taken fire, or a hurricane blown, we should have been tempted to rejoice and to hail the excitement as a boon.

[HARRIET KING], *Letters from Muskoka, By An Emigrant Lady*, 1878

There was nothing, absolutely nothing, to do. No one who has not had a like experience could appreciate even half the misery contained in these words—nothing to do. Just imagine sitting for hours in one's home doing nothing, looking out of a scrap of window and seeing nothing, searching for work and finding nothing. There were a few people at Forty-mile, but I was not acquainted with them, and at times when I thought I could not bear [for] another minute the utter blankness of such an existence I would walk to a little cemetery nearby for consolation. Even a cemetery can be pleasant under such circumstances, if only as a break in the landscape.

ETHEL BERRY in Frances Backhouse (ed.), *Women of the Klondike*, 1995

For the next two writers, it was not their own circumstances that distressed them, but their neighbours'.

Yesterday evening, tea being over, we gathered in our pleasant sitting room at about seven o'clock for prayers.

After the opening hymn, instead of proceeding as usual, dear Mr McCarthy turned to me and said that they would be glad if I would tell a little about what I knew of the condition of the thousands of factory-girls in London, and also of work being done amongst them.

I was of course much surprised at so unexpected a request, but it is never difficult, I suppose, to speak of a matter so near one's heart, and I gladly consented.

We had a long talk about it all, the dear friends seeming much interested, and it led to earnest prayer, which will, I trust, be continued. I can almost see the pleasant scene now as I write,— though it seems so long ago. The spacious room, with its freshly whitewashed walls and clean ceiling, the simple, brightly coloured texts and Chinese scrolls and map, showing up so well on their white background; dear Mary, sitting near the harmonium, and all the others (we are thirteen here just now, in Miss Murray's temporary absence) gathered in the lamplight and the quiet that comes at the close of the busy day.

In the middle of our talk, however, the pleasant, peaceful hour was suddenly broken in upon. Ah, that loud knocking on the outside door is a sadly too-familiar sound! A hurried footstep on the stair, and, yes—it is indeed as we feared! An opium case, some one must go at once. In a few minutes Miss A—— and Miss Rentfield are on their way with the messenger who came for help. They have not far to go, but we know not how long they may be, or what they may find awaiting them. The Lord go with and help them! An hour or two brought them back with their sad story. A respectable house, crowded with people. Such a young girl! She had taken a large quantity of opium, and was lying on a bed in an inner room. At first she would not take the medicines, and an awful scene ensued. Four or five people held her down, in spite of her most violent and fearful resistance, and forced the liquid between her clenched teeth. Suddenly, in answer to prayer, she gave up her struggles, and said she would take it quietly herself. This she did, sitting up, and drinking enough to cause the desired effect.

A good deal of opium was thrown up, and before they left our sisters were encouraged to hope that she would recover. A great crowd of people were present, staring in at all the doors and windows, and some of them promised to come to the 'Je-su tang' the next day, and hear more of the strange doctrine, told under such sad circumstances for the first time to some! Poor girl, it was only a quarrel with her mother that led to the desperate deed. Often, alas! it is perpetrated thus out of *revenge*, for the Chinese believe that after such a death the departed soul will haunt the living offenders, and be able to bring upon them all kinds of evil and suffering.

Alas, alas! for the dark places of the earth, where the devil *reigns*, and drives men to such awful deeds.

GERALDINE GUINNESS, *In the Far East*, [1899]

This place presents many painful proofs that the Slave Trade is not yet abandoned, as unchristian and cruel; this inhuman and brutalizing traffic is carried on here to a considerable extent: as we sat at breakfast the morning after our arrival, we saw a heavy carriage of manure pass along the public road, and through the town, drawn by human beings, with very partial covering on their bodies, and guarded and urged forward by a guide, who carried a lash in his hand, and who often used it very smartly; and this is a common sight. These oppressed creatures are generally yoked together in pairs of six or eight, according to the weight of the carriage given them to draw.

Slaves are also kept by masters of inns; and when a gig goes out, a slave is sent to run by the side, and expected to go at the same rate as the horse, and to take care that more than the allowed number do not ride at the same time.

Any persons possessing slaves, have power to send them to the Bazaar to be publicly whipped, if they have been guilty of dishonesty, or running away. Here, the treatment is sometimes very inhuman. Once as I was passing, I beheld a poor creature lying on his face, fastened to a piece of timber, and groaning most piteously. On enquiry, I found he had received fifty lashes in the morning, and was condemned to lie there till evening, when he was to have fifty more!

'Then what is man? And what man, seeing this,
And having human feelings, does not blush,
And hang his head, to think himself a man?'

KETURAH JEFFREYS, *The Widowed Missionary's Journal*, 1827

What Mrs Jeffreys could do with in Madagascar, according to the recommendation of a later missionary, Jane Moir, is a good day or two's march. Nothing like it for bracing the soul.

84

We begin to waken and call out, 'Dojimi, is the sky beginning to redden?' Dojimi calls back, 'Very, very little'; then we say, 'Make the tea,' and forthwith proceed to crawl out of our warm bed, and with all haste get into cold, half-damp clothes—no time for washing or hair dressing—and with perhaps a blanket on for a bit, open the tent door and go out into the chilly, cold grey light of the first dawn. Here we find our two canvas chairs, and little table set, and a fine wood fire to warm us, and tea and scones all ready, and while we drink our tea the camp becomes very lively. The men all get to their loads, those in charge of the tent take it down and roll it up, others fold the beds, others put the pots, and pans, and cups, and biscuits, into the big baskets they are carried in, and before six o'clock the whole sixty-one of us are ready to set out, all shivering and cold. Then we get up a shout, and all the carriers call out 'Olendo, olendo, olendo, Ru Tanganyika,' and all down the line we hear 'Olendo, olendo.' This simply means 'March, march, let us march for Tanganyika,' and they get as cheery as possible with shouting, and forget about their heavy loads, and the thick, cold dew. We usually make some of the carriers go on before so as to shake off some of this dew, which sometimes is very wetting. As a rule we are pretty well soaked in the course of half an hour, and go along in a sort of shrivelled-up state, creepy and cold, till the glorious sun rises over the horizon, and immediately we feel warm, and the whole caravan marches along single file, quickly and happily. Very soon Fred and I get to the front, as the carriers stop often to rest, and on we go, march, march, trudge, trudge, step by step, over that knoll, and across this stream, past a grassy plain, and through a long stretch of forest, on and on, a drink of water at one place, and ten minutes rest at another, till we have gone perhaps ten or twelve miles, and reach the camp, or village, where we intend to stop and have breakfast—this usually between 9 and 10 o'clock. I have found out it is so easy to say we are going to walk to Tanganyika and back—a distance of only 480 miles, but how different it is when it comes to one mile after another, to walk along sturdily for 20 minutes and remember at the end we have only made *one* mile! One has plenty of time for thought, and I find myself composing endless letters, and thinking of what I would like to write to each of the dear people at home. Fred spends his time hunting for gold. He walks along with an iron crow-bar, and breaks off pieces of rocks and stones, and gets specimens out of all the burns and water courses. These he grinds in a mortar and washes, but so far we have found no gold. Well, to get on with the day. About 10 o'clock we reach the village, very tired, hungry, and meltingly hot, for by this time the sun is high above us. We fix on a shady spot, and our boys go off and get firewood and water. In a very short time the rice pot is boiling away, and the stew is simmering . . .

Usually we set out again about 2 o'clock, and walk till 4 or 5, but we cannot go so far as we often wish, as many of the carriers have heavy loads, over sixty lbs. calico, and get tired travelling long distances, day after day. As soon as we get to camp, the tent is pitched, and the carriers settle down round it, in groups of men from different tribes. The first care of everyone is to get fire-wood, for they keep up blazing fires all night, both for warmth and also to frighten away wild beasts. They usually have from fourteen to twenty splendid fires, and we have a big one to ourselves, which is most comforting. The finest time of all the day is now, when we are resting beside the camp fire. Everyone is happy and cheery, talking and laughing, and you have no idea what a pretty sight it is. The calm sky and stars overhead, the trees, and fires, and black figures round them, *and* the porridge pots! I can't tell you how nice it is . . .

JANE MOIR, *A Lady's Letters from Central Africa*, 1891

But it did not work for everyone.

The sun was sinking. The drinks and food were far on ahead. The horses crawled along at a snail's pace, and eventually, when it was almost dark, we reached a collection of dismal and very dilapidated grass huts, which we were assured was the longed-for Dansi. The carriers had been there for about an hour, but nothing was yet unpacked and no dinner was ready, as Sulie, who was in charge of the party, was convinced that we could not intend to spend the night there. Several of the boys were sound asleep, and every one was very depressed and downhearted to find Dansi fallen so far below what we had all expected from Balu's glowing description of it. By the time we had finished a much-needed cocktail, it was pitch dark, and so huge bonfires were lighted, which soon made little patches of glory in the general gloom and cheered us all up considerably. The boys proceeded to put up the beds and to unpack what was necessary for the night, and the P. M. and I set out to make a tour of inspection of our new quarters.

The huts were small and extremely dirty, many of them having collapsed altogether. Cobwebs had festooned themselves across the doorways of those that still remained standing, and, when we brushed them aside to investigate further, snakes, lizards, and divers creeping things scuttled out into the long grass and rustled away into the silence. Huge spiders swung from the rotting roofs, and black wasps, an inch long, had nested in the walls. The floors were lumpy and uneven as though they had been recently dug up, and it is my conviction, although I fortunately did not think of it at the time, that the place had been used as a burial ground by natives, who always bury their beloved in an empty hut, either their own or that of some one else. There was a faint and curiously fetid atmosphere about the whole camp, and the water, which was brought up from the river near by, had a most evil odour and was so muddy that it was impossible to see the bottom of the bath.

At last the beds were put up and we were safely tucked inside our mosquito curtains, much too tired to care anything about the rest of our surroundings. But hardly had we dropped off to sleep, when one of the other huts caught alight and threatened to destroy the whole camp, and we were obliged to get up and sit outside on our boxes till it was safe to go back to bed again.

Enough of Dansi! It was a pestilential hole . . .

I sometimes wondered whether, after all, Nigeria was such a paradise as in my first enthusiasm I had supposed it to be. There seemed, now that I had investigated the countryside for miles round, nothing much to do; and I often found myself reflecting rather bitterly on the insignificant position of a woman in what is practically a man's country. It may be perhaps imagined that under such conditions a tendency to exaggerate her own importance would evolve in the female breast. But not at all. Very far from it. If there is one spot on earth where a woman feels of no importance

87

whatever, it is in Nigeria at the present day. She is frankly there on sufferance, and the kind-hearted man who tries to make her welcome is none the less aware of his own magnanimity in doing so. The nicer he is, the more trouble she feels herself to be; and any woman who has ever sat meekly on a seat in a crowded train while its lawful occupant sways on a strap, towering in chivalrous superiority above her, will fully understand what I mean.

At the same time, one's position has certainly the charm of novelty. Men, I thought, regarded one not as an individual but as woman incarnate, and their attitude towards one generally showed very clearly how the sex had treated them. Often, during an exchange of civilities with a strange man, have I heard him sigh plaintively to himself: 'Oh Lord, here she is again. Is there no corner of the earth where a chap may hide himself and be at peace?' One man would beam a glad smile of welcome for the sake of a wife who might be encouraged by one's example to join him; and another dart a glance of active dislike for exactly the same reason. Some were hard and cynical, their pride still smarting where a woman's hand had hurt it; others, patient and sad of eye, looked as though the sight of one made their hearts ache more than usual. I saw a great many aching hearts in Nigeria, and I believe that nine men out of every ten are there to get away from some woman, either for her good or their own.

MRS HORACE TREMLETT, *With the Tin Gods*, 1915

SIX

MATTERS DOMESTIC

It is rather dangerous to take English servants to the United States;
there are very few whose attachment and good sense are proof against
the tempting charms and delusions of nominal equality.
Mrs Houstoun, *Texas and the Gulf of Mexico*, 1844

*I*t must have been difficult for a conscientious lady like Mrs
Houstoun: on the one hand, she had a moral and social obligation to keep servants in their place. God forbid they should
become corrupted with this American notion of domestic democ-
racy: people like her had a duty to protect simple souls from such
inconvenient 'charms and delusions'. Yet, she knew that, for an
emigrant British gentlewoman, emigrant British servants were
essential. And in cripplingly short supply. Not just for gentlewomen, either: if there is one theme that unites all the material
I have seen in the making of this book, it must be that of domestic help, and the hopes, pressures, satisfaction, or desperation it
involves.

So how could the right sort of servant (and lots of them) be
encouraged?

The philanthropist Caroline Chisholm had the best idea. After
a distressing visit to Australia in 1838, during which she witnessed
literally hundreds of young women seeking work by wandering
aimlessly and dangerously around Sydney, she established an
agency. She housed the girls first in wholesome hostels or 'depots'
along the coast of New South Wales, then placed them in previ-
ously approved households, keeping in touch thereafter. 'The
emigrants' friend', they called her, or 'our Moses in bonnet and
shawl'. Those women who enlisted with her were lucky.

Others had to make do, more chancily, with placing or answering advertisements in emigrant papers, or even with speculating that a passage taken 'blind' on an emigrant ship would lead to health, wealth, and happiness. Or, at least, a job for a while.

Of course none of these methods of brokering domestic help guaranteed *success for either party, and there were alternatives for desperate householders: they could take on local staff (there is advice here on how to manage native servants), or they could do the work themselves (see the household and culinary hints . . .). Most, of necessity, did the latter, and this chapter finds several shifting virtuosically for themselves—especially the astonishing Mary Walker—and even relishing the challenge of Empire-buildings from the kitchen sink. Wives, after all, were the best and cheapest domestic staff of the lot.*

THE LADIES' COLUMN

1.—There is an unlimited demand for wives of all ranks, from the shepherd to the gentleman squatter, with his 1,000 head of cattle, and 20,000 sheep. The Colonists, as a body, whether emigrants or native born, make good husbands, kind, indulgent, and generous. They are all rather rough in their language to each other, but no one ever heard of a Bushman beating his wife. In the towns there is as much gaiety as in England. Rather more. The Bush huts have not generally been very comfortable; but there is no reason why they should not be as well built and furnished as in English farm houses. Young widows and orphans of small means will find themselves in reality much safer in an Australian town than in any of the great towns of Europe, better protected, and with better prospects. Of course some caution is necessary before accepting the first offers made, but there is very little difficulty in finding out an Australian settler's character. There are obvious advantages in two or more ladies joining to make a party for the sea-voyage, besides reasons of economy. There can be no more impropriety in going to Australia than to India for the same purpose.

Adelaide is at present the best port for young ladies, as there is a committee of ladies there who receive and protect female emigrants.

For Governesses, there is a moderate demand. We should only recommend those to think of emigration who are not comfortable here. Every lady thinking of emigrating should know how to bake, boil, roast, wash, and iron, and then although she may not have to do these things, she will feel independent.

For Domestic and Farm-servants the demand is unlimited, and will so continue for many years, as a good sober cook, housemaid, or nurse, is worth any wages, and may always have a house of her own within twelve months. A clever maid-servant is sure to better her position by emigrating to Australia, and will frequently save part of the passage-money by attending on one of the lady passengers.

Never stand out for high wages at first. Get a house over your head, and then change if you can for the better.

Country girls, Irish and others, not able to become domestic servants, would make excellent shepherdesses. All dry flocks, that is, not breeding ewes, will be under the charge of women, whenever an equality of sexes has been produced by copious female emigration.

Sidney's Emigrant's Journal, 1848

WANTED, by a respectable young married woman, SITUATION as WET-NURSE, milk three weeks old. Apply 43 Charles-street, Fitzroy.

LADY (young) wishes SITUATION as BARMAID, sings and plays the pianoforte. Address Alice, Argus office.

JUNCTION REGISTRY Office, St. Kilda.—COOKS, Laundresses, General Servants, House Parlour Maids, experienced Nurses Waiting engagement.

BARMAID (pianiste), country town, 20s; Companion, good pianiste, hotel. Registry-office, 58 Little Collins-street east.

REQUIRED, superior NURSE and Needlewoman, Protestant. Best references required. Apply, Saturday and Monday, to Mrs Hartley Williams, Kenly, Boundary-road, Toorak.

WANTED, SITUATION, not menial, as COMPANION to an invalid, teach
Children. Junction Registry Office, St. Kilda.
WIDOW, well educated, respectable, and experienced, desires RE-
ENGAGEMENT as HOUSEKEEPER. Excellent references. Anxious,
Argus office.

Melbourne Argus, 1880

Dear Madam, I seen your 'ad.' in the *Province*. I have 100 and 20
acres of my hone, it is all payed for. I lost my wife 4 years ago I ham
36 years of age I have horses and cattle and a lot of chicken. Would
you care to go in Pardners with me as I want to settle down again.
Pleas let me know by return mail.

ELLA SYKES, *A Home Help in Canada*, 1912

Agency owner Caroline Chisholm was thankfully more circum-
spect in finding positions for her girls.

My object was always to get one placed [at a time]. I never
attempted more than one at first. Having succeeded in getting one
female servant in a neighbourhood, I used to leave the feeling to
spread. The first thing that gave me the idea that I could work in
this manner was this: with some persuasion I induced a man to take
a servant, who said that it would be making a fine lady of his wife.
However, I spoke to him and told him the years his wife had been
labouring for him; this had the desired effect. The following morning I was told by a neighbouring settler: 'You are quite upsetting
the settlement, Mrs Chisholm: my wife is uncommonly cross this
morning; she says she is as good as her neighbour, and she must
have a servant; and I think she has as much right to one.' It was
amongst that class that the girls eventually married best. If they
married one of the sons, the father and mother would be thankful;
if not, they would be protected as members of the family. They
slept in the same room with their own daughters.

Sidney's Emigrant's Journal, 1848

Many, especially at the West, report the customary position of [domestic] girls in the family as that of daughters, sitting at the same table, dressing as well or better, riding to the village to church in the same vehicle, and say that they appear to many even quicker than the ladies [to marry]. The tendency throughout the West to *immediate marriage* is a subject of general complaint. One gentleman counts over his girls on his fingers with this curious statistical result: 'In the last eight years I have had in my employ 23 girls, 19 of whom have married out of my house.'

VERE FOSTER, *Work and Wages; or, the Penny Emigrant's Guide*, 1855

There is an error which female servants are very apt to fall into in this country, which, as a true friend, I would guard them against committing. This is adopting a free and easy manner, often bordering upon impertinence, towards their employers. They are apt to think that because they are entitled to a higher rate of wages, they are not bound to render their mistresses the same respect of manners as was usual in the old country. Now, as they receive more, they ought not to be less thankful to those who pay them well, and should be equally zealous in doing their duty. They should bear in mind that they are commanded to render 'honour to whom honour is due.' A female servant in Canada, whose manners are respectful and well-behaved, will always be treated with consideration and even with affection. After all, good-breeding is as charming a trait in a servant as it is in a lady. Were there more of that kindly feeling existing between the upper and lower classes, both parties would be benefited, and a bond of union established, which would extend beyond the duration of a few months or a few years, and be continued through life: how much more satisfactory than that unloving strife where the mistress is haughty and the servant insolent.

CATHERINE TRAILL, *The Canadian Settler's Guide*, 1860

LIST OF EMIGRANTS
[The Female Middle Class Emigration Society]

No.	Destination	Date	Salary	Remarks
1	Australia	1861	£70	Was nursery governess in England at £20 per annum.
2			—	Very young and inexperienced, obtained situation after a time.
4			£35	The climate caused severe headaches, which much affected her success.
5			—	Married directly, and returned to England.
7	Africa		£24	Obtained situation shortly, very comfortable and happy.
11	Australia		£60	Had experienced great difficulty in obtaining employment in England, on account of slight deafness.
14			—	Obtained situation as shopwoman, but lost it through mis-conduct.
20		1862	£30	Two situations offered on landing, married after six months.
21			—	Nothing known.
23	Australia		—	Not at all successful, too old for adaptation to a new scene.

From *New Horizons: A Hundred Years of Women's Migration*,
1963

I am very glad I came to Australia, but I cannot say I like it very much. It is such an out of the world place, and so monotonous, but as far as the treatment goes I could not meet with nor desire kinder. With no one in this neighbourhood have I seen the social distinction made with Governesses that there is at home. I have very little work here in comparison with London. I do not think £80 per annum here as much as £60 at home, dress is very expensive, and the people are dressy. You will be glad to hear that my pupil has

94

made great progress in all her studies, but particularly in music, which pleases Mrs Hines very much. They brought out a very nice piano, in fact 'Bush life' is a strange mixture of roughing it and refinement . . . Literature is much more brought forward here, in the general way, than at home, because there are no new daily topics. The standing one is sheep, in which ladies take no part, of course.

LOUISA GEOGHEGAN [Victoria, 1867] in *New Horizons: A Hundred Years of Women's Migration*, 1963

Luxor, February 15 1866. Dearest Mother. I am sorry to say that Marie has become so excessively bored, dissatisfied, and, she says, ill, that I am going to send her back rather than be worried so—and *damit hats eine ende* [and that's the end] of European maids. Of course an ignorant girl *must* be bored to death here—a land of no amusements and no flirtation *is* unbearable.

I shall borrow a slave of a friend here, an old black woman who is quite able and more than willing to serve me, and when I go down to Cairo I will get either a *ci-devant* slave or an elderly Arab woman. Dr Patterson strongly advised me do to so last year. He has one who has been thirteen years his housekeeper, an old Beduin, I believe, and as I now am no longer looked upon as a foreigner, I shall be able to get a respectable Arab woman, a widow or a divorced woman of a certain age who will be too happy to have 'a good home', as our maids say. I shall be taken good care of if I fall ill, much better than I should get from a European in a sulky frame of mind . . .

Marie's idea of happiness is a rollicking hotel life such as, I fancy, she had at Spa. If I had known she had been servant in an hotel at a German watering place, I would not have taken her. She is thoroughly cunning and boundlessly wasteful and greedy. I only say this for your information in case you should think of taking her. You know I hate rows and allow her to say that she leaves me of her own accord, which is, indeed, true. She is mad with impatience to be gone.

LADY LUCIE DUFF GORDON, *Last Letters from Egypt*, 1875

When a female transport-ship arrives at Sydney, all the madams on board occupy the few days which elapse before their landing, in preparing to produce the most dazzling effect at their *descent* upon the Australian shore.

With rich silk dresses,—bonnets *a-la-mode*,—ear pendents three inches long,—gorgeous shawls and splendid veils,—silk stockings, kid gloves, and parasols in hand, dispensing sweet odours from their profusely perfumed forms, they disembark, and are assigned as *servants*, and distributed to the expectant settlers . . . The hapless settler, who expected a *servant*, able, or at least willing, to act, perhaps, both as house and dairy-maid, finds he has received quite a *princess*!

Her *highness*, with her gloved and delicate fingers, can do *no* sort of work!

JAMES MUDIE, *The Felonry of New South Wales*, 1837

There was one sort of work hardly anyone here could avoid, however. The chores of childcare involved mothers and staff, neighbours and family, alike.

I have just returned from a country case—nine of us in a tiny bungalow, three beds among the lot. I slept on a broken-springed sofa, rolled up in a blanket. The entire family washed in a tin dipper in the kitchen, and used the same water and the same towel and the same brush and comb until I went there. Open windows were unknown, and the house was as hot as the nether regions. The children were unkempt and spoiled; the food mostly fried potatoes . . . Now, if you can absolutely conceal your distaste and walk tactfully, you may do a lot. I taught those children to say 'please' and 'thank you', to wash before meals . . . and I learned to cook and wash quite creditably. I know they were sorry to part with me. I cleaned the house till it shone like a new pin, and I was resolutely cheerful, in spite of the fact that my heart was in my boots. I just set my teeth and made up my mind that I was going to see the thing through, and at night, when the children were in bed, and I had made a tray of cocoa ready for my patient and her husband, I used to go out into the back yard. Underfoot lay potato peelings and empty tin cans, but overhead, by the grace of God, the exceeding beauty of the stars; and, tired but well content with the day's work, I used to return to my broken-backed sofa and sleep as long as the baby would let me . . .

[ANON. (a maternity nurse in Alberta, 1913)] in *New Horizons: A Hundred Years of Women's Migration*, 1963

By this time my condition became apparent to the most casual observer. Frequently the squaws approached me and patting me on the bosom, would say, 'By and by papoose.' The urgent need of some new maternity gowns appealed to me every day. But where was I to procure them, hundreds of miles from any dry goods emporium? Before starting on the journey I had made, to protect it from the dust of travel, a stout covering of blue plaid gingham for my feather bed. This outer covering I had removed when I sold the bed in Salt Lake. Ripping open the plain, straight seams, I cut and fashioned . . . a comfortable, if not stylish garment, making it by hand at odd moments in camp or as I rode along on my way. From a big flowered dressing gown that my husband had discarded as being too effeminate to be worn on the plains . . . I made another suitable and befitting dress, although the colouring was almost too gaudy and gay for that style of garment.

LAVINIA HONEYMAN PORTER, *By Ox Team to California*, 1910

Rose about five. Had breakfast. Got my housework done about nine. Baked six loaves of bread. Made a kettle of mush and have now a suet pudding and beef boiling. I have managed to put my house in order . . . Nine o'clock p.m. was delivered of another son.

MARY WALKER, *Diary* [n.d.]

For Mary Walker, childbirth was obviously all in a day's work.
Which is really what this chapter is all about.

We have fallen into it (the life) wonderfully quickly; completely
sunk the lady and become sort of maids-of-all-work. Our day
begins soon after 6 o'clock by laying the breakfast, skimming the
cream, whilst our woman is frying bacon and making the porridge
for the breakfast at 6.30. Mr B—— and A—— are out by 5
o'clock, in order to water, feed, and harness their horses all ready
to go out at 7 o'clock, when we get rid of all the men. We then make
the beds, help in the washing-up, clean the knives, and this morning I undertook the dinner, and washed out some of the clothes, as
we have not been able to find a towel, duster, or glass-cloth, whilst
Mrs G—— cleaned out the dining-room. The dirt of the house is,
to our minds, appalling; but as Mrs G—— only arrived a few days
before we did, and all the winter the four men were what is called
in this country 'baching it' (from bachelor), namely, having to do
everything for themselves, it is, perhaps, not surprising that the
floors are rather dirty and that there is a little dust. The weather is
much against our cleaning, as the mud sticks to the boots and, do
what you will, it is almost impossible to get it off; not that the men
seem to have thought much about it, as, until we arrived and
suggested it, there was no scraper to either door. Poor Mr B——
was rather hurt in his feelings this morning on expressing some
lament at the late sharp frosts, that all his cabbages would be killed,
when we said that it was a pity he had sown them out of doors, as
he might almost have grown them on the dining-room carpet. He
also amuses us by lamenting that he did so much cleaning and
washed the floors so often; he might just as well have left it until we
arrived. Our time is well filled up until dinner, at 12.30, at which
we have such ravenous appetites, we are told, no profits made on
the farm will pay our keep. At half-past 1 when the men turn out
again, we generally go out with them, and some out-door occupation is found for us; either driving the waggons or any other jobs.
There is a lot of hay littered about, and that has to be stacked; also
the waste straw or rubbish which is burnt, and the fires have to be
made up. Three-quarters of an hour before either dinner or supper
(the latter meal is about half-past 6) a flag, the Union Jack, is

hoisted at the end of the farther stable—if neither A—— nor Mr
B—— is about, we undertake to do it—to call the men in; and they
declare the horses see the flag as soon as they do and stop directly.

MRS CECIL HALL, *A Lady's Life on a Farm in Manitoba*,
1884

1. bild fire in back yard to het kettle of rain water.
2. set tubs so smoke won't blow in eyes if wind is peart.
3. shave 1 hole cake lie sope in bilin water.
4. sort things. make 3 piles. 1 pile white, 1 pile cullord, 1 pile
work briches and rags.
5. stur flour in cold water to smooth then thin down with bilin
water [for starch]
6. rub dirty spots on board. scrub hard. then bile. rub cullord
but don't bile just rench and starch.
7. take white things out of kettle with broom stick handel then
rench, blew and starch
8. pore rench water in flower bed.
9. scrub porch with hot sopy water
10. turn tubs upside down
11. go put on a cleen dress, smooth hair with side combs, brew
cup of tee, set and rest and rock a spell and count blessings.

from SANDRA MYRES, *Westering Women*, 1982

The daily household duties to be performed by every lady are
much the same in India as elsewhere. After breakfast the khán-
sámán has to be interviewed as before described, his previous day's
bill looked over, checked, and paid, arrangements made for any
extra things required, &c. Then will come a visit to the 'go-downs'
(store cupboards), which will most likely be in the verandah. From
them you will give out all that is required for the day by the cook,
the bearer, the khitmutgar, and the syces; the groceries for kitchen
use, the oil for the lamps, corn (gram) for the horses, cows, or
goats, if you keep them—for corn of all kinds should always be

kept under lock and key, and given out daily as required, or else you will find it lasts but little time. This duty over, you will most likely see that your tailor (durzee) is supplied with the work you require him to do during the day. You will give a look round the different rooms to see that the proper amount of dusting has been done, and by that time you will be very glad to rest awhile, and read or write, until it is time for tiffin.

'AN ANGLO-INDIAN', *Indian Outfits and Establishments*, 1882

January 11, 1839. The most comfortable thing today is that I have a very nice baking, and there is nothing that affects the spirits more than the well or ill rising of your bread. Our servant of last year, Mary, blessed with most admirable spirits, if her bread would not rise was the most melancholy creature imaginable. I quite understand it, now that the bread is my department.

ANN LANGTON, *A Gentlewoman in Upper Canada*, ed. H. H. Langton, 1950

Yeast. 1lb. each sugar, flour and potatoes; 2 ozs. each hops and salt; 1 gallon water. Boil for an hour the hops and water, strain, and set by to cool. Boil the potatoes in 1 pt. water; mash them very smooth, and mix them with the water they were boiled in. Put in a large basin the sugar, flour, and salt; mix with them very gradually the mashed potatoes and hop-water. Bottle, cork tightly, tying on the corks with string. It will be ready in 24 hours.

ADELA B. STEWART, *My Simple Life in New Zealand*, 1908

I have been engaged this afternoon making up my remaining store of tallow into four dozen portly-looking dips, eight to the pound. My last making was twelve dozen, and I think the larger number is very much as quickly accomplished as the smaller one, for they gather more tallow when thoroughly cooled, so that with many I need not go through them so often as with few. Now that I know how to manage the matter I find it positively a cleanly operation. Mary looked horrified when I set up my apparatus in the kitchen, which had just received its Saturday polish, but I do not think she found it a bit worse when I had packed away my things again. The two elder ladies were still very busy upholstering. I do not think any ladies on the lake have better fitting garments than our two arm-chairs.

ANN LANGTON, *A Gentlewoman in Upper Canada*, ed. H. H. Langton, 1950

N.B. When a chimney wants sweeping in the Karroo, the usual mode of procedure is to send a fowl down it.

ANNIE MARTIN, *Home Life on an Ostrich Farm*, 1890

During the fall of '35, I was assisting my husband in taking up a crop of potatoes, in the field, and observing a vast number of fine dandelion roots among the potatoes, it brought the dandelion coffee back to my memory, and I determined to try some for our supper. Without saying anything to my husband, I threw aside some of the roots, and when we left work, collecting a sufficient quantity for the experiment, I carefully washed the roots quite clean, without depriving them of the fine brown skin which covers them, and which contains the aromatic flavour, which so nearly resembles coffee that it is difficult to distinguish it from it while roasting.

I cut my roots into small pieces, the size of a kidney-bean, and roasted them on an iron baking-pan in the stove-oven, until they were as brown and crisp as coffee. I then ground and transferred a small cupful of the powder to the coffee-pot, pouring upon it scalding water, and boiling it for a few minutes briskly over the fire. The result was beyond my expectations. The coffee proved excellent—far superior to the common coffee we procured at the stores.

Few of our colonists are acquainted with the many uses to which this neglected but most valuable plant may be applied. I will point out a few which have come under my own observation, convinced as I am that the time will come when this hardy weed, with its golden flowers and curious seed-vessels, which form a constant plaything to the little children rolling about and luxuriating among the grass, in the sunny month of May, will be transplanted into our gardens and tended with due care.

The dandelion planted in trenches, and blanched to a beautiful cream-colour with straw, makes an excellent salad, quite equal to endive, and is more hardy and requires less care.

In many parts of the United States, particularly in new districts where vegetables are scarce, it is used early in the spring, and boiled with pork as a substitute for cabbage. During our residence in the bush we found it, in the early part of May, a great addition to the dinner-table. In the township of Dummer, the settlers boil the tops, and add hops to the liquor, which they ferment, and from which they obtain excellent beer. I have never tasted this simple beverage, but I have been told by those who use it that it is equal to the table-beer used at home.

SUSANNA MOODIE, *Roughing it in the Bush*, 1852

The orthodox material here is of course kangaroo, a piece of which is divided nicely into cutlets two or three inches broad and a third of an inch thick. The next requisite is a straight clean stick, about four feet long, sharpened at both ends. On the narrow part of this, for the space of a foot or more, the cutlets are spitted at intervals, and on the end is placed a piece of delicately rosy fat bacon. The strong end of the stick-spit is now stuck fast and erect in the ground, close by the fire, to leeward; care being taken that it does not burn. Then the bacon on the summit of the spit, speedily softening in the genial blaze, drops a lubricating shower of rich and savoury tears on the leaner kangaroo cutlets below, which forthwith frizzle and steam and sputter with as much ado as if they were illustrious Christmas beef grilling in some London chop-house under the gratified nose of the expectant consumer. 'And gentleman,' as dear old Hardcastle would have said, if he had dined with us in the bush, 'to men that are hungry, stuck-up kangaroo and bacon are very good eating.' Kangaroo is, in fact, very like hare.

LOUISA MEREDITH, *My Home in Tasmania*, 1852

No Lady need ever be ashamed of knowing how to cook, but I must say, that there is every excuse for allowing her talents in that line, to lie dormant, if she has to stand over a hot fire; but in this little stove that drawback is quite superseded, for the most delicate could stand, or even sit, if she chose, and superintend her own little fancy dishes.

[ANON.] *Every Lady her Own Cook: The Patent Crimean Cooking Stove*, 1857

MENUS FOR FAMILY DINNERS

No. 1.
Oxtail Soup.
Steak and Kidney Pudding.
Roast Leg of Mutton (with Red Currant Jelly).
Bread Pudding.   Fruit Tart.
Cheese Fritters.

No. 2.
Boiled Fish with Oyster Sauce.
Steak and Kidney Pie.
Cold Lamb and Salad.
Raspberry Cream and Cocoanut Pudding.
Whipped Cream.
Cheese Sandwiches.

No. 3.
Artichoke Purée.
Chicken Pie.
Roast Rolled Beef (with Baked Potatoes).
Plum Pudding.   Fruit Salad.
(with Sauce).   Whipped Cream.

No. 4.
Oysters on Toast.
Veal and Macaroni Shape.
Roast Sirloin of Beef (with Horse Radish Sauce).
Cream Cup Puddings (with Custard Sauce).
Vanilla Cream Puffs.
Dessert.

No. 5.
Pea Soup.
Fricassée of Calf's Head.
Rolled Loin of Mutton.
Russell Pudding.   Pancakes.
Cheese.   Celery.   Biscuits.

No. 6.
Fried Flounders.
Lamb's Cutlets and Green Peas.
Cold Beef and Salad.
Lemon Cornflour.   Stewed Prunes.
Cheese Fondu.

No. 7.
White Soup.
Boiled Cod and Oyster Sauce.
Veal and Ham Pie.
Roast Forequarter of Lamb.
Peach Pudding.   Vanilla Soufflé.
Mayonnaise of Chicken.
Dessert.

[ANON.] *Colonial Everyday Cookery*, [1912]

H. and I went out for a walk together, and having learnt a few
words of Arabic I ordered breakfast for our return. On entering
the dining-room later we found one egg reposing exactly in the
middle of the table, and arranged around it one spoon, one

knife, one fork. Nothing else at all, not even a tablecloth on the bare oak.

E. L. BUTCHER, *Egypt As We Knew It*, 1911

About ayahs in particular, I have heard most lamentable accounts—what lying, cheating, thieving creatures they were—in short, a 'thorough bad lot;' but I know how often in England I had heard the whole class of servants abused, often without rhyme or reason, and so turned rather a deaf ear to my would-be counsellors. I was very particular about my ayah's character, and I saw the lady she had lived with; she was by no means blind to her faults, but still gave her a fair character. She remained with me all the time I was in India, travelled over a thousand miles down country with us to Bombay, and only took leave when we went on board, even coming with us on the ship to see where 'missee Baba,' my little girl, her especial charge, would sleep, and then shed floods of tears at parting. From that woman I had every possible attention.

'AN ANGLO-INDIAN', *Indian Outfits and Establishments*, 1882

One word of advice to housekeepers, masculine and feminine—*don't* beat the boys. There is still a prevailing idea that the master who wields the *bulala* (whip) with most vigour gets best served. But this I beg leave to doubt.

CONSTANCE LARYMORE, *A Resident's Wife in Nigeria*, 1908

Before starting from your English home, go to your village black-smith, don his apron, and tinker and toil with him as much as he will let you, till you get a good notion of his trade. Go to your wheel-wright, and get him to show you his trick of straightening a bent axle, how to box one, how to cure its crookedness, and to heal wheel illnesses generally. Haunt the bench of your neighbouring carpenter, till you get a wrinkle or two from him. Even your butcher and your baker might tell you something, that you may thank them for when thousands of miles away from them. Be a Jack-of-all-trades, with more than a smattering of knowledge of each, and you will save your pocket as well as your patience thereby. You *may* get Kafir labour in plenty, but you may also have to go for weeks without any. The servant-market is liable to fluctuations, and it is well to be independent thereof. White servants you will never have. Even if your social status in the old country be that of servitude (ever honourable), yet I venture to predict you will, like your neighbours, soon after arrival, be ordering about your 'boys,' and telling them to do in South Africa, what in England you would 'think it shame' to see any one doing for you but yourself. Your wife, good, hard-working soul, who in her old home would slave at her washtub and scrub her floors cheerfully; here, if she be so lucky as to have floors at all, will make that lazy 'Jim,' or that provoking 'Oomfan' clean them for her.

If only a band of sensible emigrants would come to this country, prepared to use their own hands, as if no black labour were to be had, they would reap riches . . .

HARRIET ROCHE, *On Trek in the Transvaal*, 1878

This winter we have gone through what at home would have half killed us. We were nearly five months without a drop of milk. The children living on salt meat and potatoes for dinner; their breakfast and supper being very weak tea and bread. Sometimes I give them boiled rice or barley, but not very often. I drink nothing but tea for I cannot touch 'punch' which is our only other beverage.

Now I am doing work to which I never was accustomed; cooking, washing, nursing, house-cleaning, etc., and I am able for all.

FRANCES STEWART, *Our Forest Home*, 1902

c/o Mrs Richmond
Albion Hall
Blythe Post Office
Ontario, Canada

My Dear Rose, I hope you are all well as ever . . . Where did you get to when you had your day off. I wish you could have come here to see me . . . Dear Rose, you would not know whether this was Sutton if there where a few more houses and a shop, Dear Girl [it] would not be any use to come and try after a place where we are as there are only a few houses here and the Mrs do there work thereselves. I dont think that you would like to milk cows well I should not care about it anyway. Dont think that I am saying this because I dont whant you to come because it would be just grand for us to be together again. You asked me whether I was sorry I went. Well, in lots and lots of things I am, no fish and potatoes, no mutton . . . cant get sweets, no cabbage, havent had any potatoes for weeks . . . How we miss our fish and potatoes, but no use grumbling; of course the fruit [is] alright and there are a lot of apples here but to tell you the truth I would much rather been at [home] than here . . .

[MS letter, unsigned, n.d.]

SEVEN

TRIUMPH AND DELIGHT

In vain did I carry a revolver till it wore a hole in my coat pocket; no armed savage threatened to kidnap me, they were only too anxious to get out of my way. And sometimes I asked myself in despair—where were the dangers and hardships that I had come out with so much fortitude to meet?

Mrs Horace Tremlett, *With the Tin Gods*, 1915

She sounds quite disappointed. It was an 'Emigrant Lady' from Muskoka a couple of chapters ago who said that she used to long for things to happen: things like bears leaping through the window, or hurricanes blowing, just to break the lonely tedium of being an emigrant Englishwoman in the back-woods. Dangers and hardships certainly make for thrilling read-ing, and it is tempting when compiling a collection like this to dwell on the hair-raising episodes and ignore the rest. So, this chapter is dedicated solely to the triumphs and delights of emigrant life.

Some are simple pleasures: the cultivation, preparation and enjoyment of the fruits of one's own piece of land; the satisfac-tion of a day's hay-mowing; falling uncomplicatedly in love. Others are more sophisticated. In fact, I should think it is hard to get much more sophisticated than enjoying a Thursday after-noon's round at the Royal Hong Kong Golf Club, unless it is presiding over the committee of the Literary Society (or the Horticultural or Musical or Benevolent Aid Societies . . .) of Canterbury, New Zealand.

The chapter begins with particular triumphs: a group of women savouring a new-found sense of independence when, perhaps for the first time in their lives, they started working for a living. A journalist, a doctor, and a missionary speak first.

The dearth of educated and intelligent people is so great at present that to get a billet needing these qualifications is as easy as saying 'knife,' and when I called at the *Morning Sun* offices haphazard and asked to be made their Social Editress, my breath was taken away by the Editor (a charming man) rushing in his shirtsleeves out of a cardboard compartment he sat in, and saying 'Certainly! Certainly! And may I ask what salary?'

This was so different to London. I stared.

Nellie remained half-way down the stairs, hidden, but could hear all, and gave me advice in stage whispers.

'Pile it on, Ma'am,' came wafting up now; 'don't be shy. Say fifty quid a month, and don't blush.'

'Er—would thirty pounds a month be too high?' I enquired, holding my breath so as not to blush.

'Not at all. We should not expect you to work for less.'

'And you're lucky to get her for that,' came on the breeze, 'a officer's wife and all! a-goin' in and out of Jo-hannesburg Society what ain't fit to black her boots!'

'Pray sit down. How do you like Africa?' said the Editor, after listening to these sounds and deciding they didn't belong to me.

'I like it, thank you. What would my duties be?'

'Oh, the ordinary duties of a Social Editress.'

I longed to enquire what these were, but thought wiser not.

'Papers differ so,' said I, sagely, 'and I expect Johannesburg is very different to London . . .'

'No, we run papers the same way as in England. You will attend all Social Functions, all the Theatres, Amateur Theatricals, Concerts, Bazaars, At Homes, Weddings, Funerals, Foundation Stones, Maternity Homes, Orphan Homes, Famous Preachers, Lectures, Millinery Shows, Stocktaking in the Shops, Sale Displays, Christmas and Easter Bazaars, Garden-parties, Masonic Lodge Nights, Balls, Dances, Hops, Cinderellas, Y.M.C.A. Teas, Eisteddfods. . . .'

'Hold hard,' said Nellie, 'you don't expect one person to do all that for thirty pounds a month?'

'We also shall expect you to do the Review Column—about six novels a week. You need only read the first and last pages. And you will also write the special Woman's Page of our Saturday issue, consisting of twelve columns upon complexions, hair-washes, underlinen, etiquette, babies, matrimony, and conundrums.'

MRS FRED MATURIN, *Petticoat Pilgrims on Trek*, 1909

February 27, 1902. I have just come from the banks of the Tigris, after seeing Dr Sutton and his family float down on their raft towards Baghdad. And now Miss Martin and myself are the only missionaries, and the only Europeans in Mosul. Three months alone! I am left in charge of the dispensary. I have 'shut out' the men, and shall only allow women and children to attend . . .

March 17. Today 200 women appeared . . . We had to turn away 150, and what a lot of crying, and pushing that required. It is difficult now to walk through the streets without being stopped by patients . . . What a difference there is now to the way I am treated! Those jeers and rude shouts and unpleasant remarks have all stopped . . . I hope those stones will be stopped too, for I have been hurt on arms, legs, and head by great boys, and the latter blows would have been serious had I not been wearing my helmet. Well, thank God, that is over now. I am the 'doctor'—magic word!

MISS BUTLIN in *Mercy and Truth*, 1903

Soon a crowd collects: the usual crowd, without which it is almost impossible to do anything, or go anywhere in China in my brief experience, at least. The people all seem kind and friendly: but, of course, intensely wondering and curious. We go straight to the inn, but long before we can reach it are escorted by a couple of hundred people at least, mostly men. Will the inn-keeper receive us with such a body-guard? It seems more than doubtful! Chang-sien-seng knows him slightly, and, while we wait outside, he goes in to explain who and what we are, and why we come. Meanwhile we sell books and the crowd gets larger. After a brief delay it appears, thank God, that the inn-people are willing; they invite us to enter the courtyard, barrows and all. This we do in the hope of getting a little rest and refreshment before going out into the city for the evening's work. Alas, vain hope!

By no means to be restrained, the crowd breaks in after us, and in a moment or two the whole courtyard is filled from end to end. For half an hour or so, L—— tries to speak, but the noise is so great that only those quite near us can hear. At last Chang-sien-seng tells us that we must, if possible, go and show ourselves in the city, for the numbers collecting outside, who cannot get in, are urgent in their desire to see us. So, commending ourselves to the Lord, we comply with this request, and, with considerable difficulty, make our way out into the narrow street. Avoiding the busiest parts, we walk up and down the city, until the dusk of evening compels us again to seek the shelter of our friendly inn. We cannot stop long in any place because of the great throngs, but pausing at some street corner or open place now and then, we get opportunity to speak a little to the woman. Some of them are so kind and nice. One, a bright-looking, middle-aged woman, takes my hand and holds it all the time we are standing talking to her, and whenever the crowd surges up roughly, presses it kindly as much as to say, 'Don't be afraid.'

To our surprise, when we reach the inn and tell the people how tired we are, and how much we long for a little quiet, they fall back from the doorway, and we go in alone, promising to come out again when [we] have had our evening meal. The women of the inn receive us most kindly and conduct us across the courtyard to the room at the back, where, with thankful hearts, we fall upon our knees beside the Chinese table, to praise God for all His gracious care of us and for the quiet moment of rest He has given. But alas! the quiet is but brief. Ere we can rise from our knees the outer doors are again thrown open, and the crowd streams in. We are again surrounded, but this time in our room, and there seems no possibility of getting supper even when it is ready. L—— speaks all the time to the changing groups about the door, and we sell many Gospels.

GERALDINE GUINNESS, *In the Far East*, [1889]

To Miss Guinness and her companions, selling Gospels to the Chinese meant success. That was why she was there.

Among the things I learned to do was the way to run a mowing-machine. It cost me many bitter tears because I got sunburned, and my hands were hard, rough, and stained with machine oil, and I used to wonder how any Prince Charming could overlook all that in any girl he came to. For all I had ever read of the Prince had to do with his 'reverently kissing her lily-white hand,' or doing some other fool trick with a hand as white as a snowflake. Well, when my Prince showed up he didn't lose much time in letting me know that 'Barkis was willing,' and I wrapped my hands in my old checked apron and took him up before he could catch his breath. Then there was no more mowing, and I almost forgot that I knew how until Mr Stewart got into such a panic. If he put a man to mow, it kept them all idle at the stacker, and he just couldn't get enough men. I was afraid to tell him I could mow for fear he would forbid me to do so. But one morning, when he was chasing a last hope of help, I went down to the barn, took out the horses, and went to mowing. I had enough cut before he got back to show him I knew how, and as he came back manless he was delighted as well as surprised. I was glad because I really like to mow, and besides that, I am adding feathers to my cap in a surprising way. When you see me again you will think I am wearing a feather duster, but it is only that I have been said to have almost as much sense as a 'mon,' and that is an honor I never aspired to, even in my wildest dreams.

ELINORE PRUITT STEWART, *Letters of a Woman Homesteader*, 1914

Sydney, December 28th, 1848

Dear Sister and Brother,—This comes with our kind love to all, hoping to find you all well as it leaves us at this time, thank God for it, dear sister. I gave birth to a little girl on the 21st of this month. I was up to dinner on Christmas-day; I have had such a good time, the babe is quite well. Martha often talks about her aunt Susan. She is such a funny little girl, and is so well. Betsy and Robert send

their kind love to John and Ann and all friends. They are quite
well, dear sister. I felt the sea-sickness very much the first part of
our voyage; I was very ill for three weeks. Martha was very poorly,
the doctor gave her porter and everything she needed. Reuben was
ill from a cold. Betsy and Robert felt very little of sickness. We had
180 miles to go by land when we got to Sydney. We were three
weeks before we got to our journey's end. Three families went up
the country with us, but not to the same place. You would never
forget the mountains and hills if you was to see them. We made our
beds on the ground every night we travelled. The children often
used to say what would aunt think if she was to see us. We are
living in a pleasant part of the country; we have got a very good
place, we live near the farm, we have plenty to eat and drink, we
grind our own corn, we have new milk every morning, we have
about twenty pounds of meat a week, half a pound of tea a week,
and very often send down a shoulder or a leg of mutton, and when
they kill a beast they give me a leg of beef to make soup, and half
the heart and kidneys for supper; we have three pounds of sugar a
week, and what we want more; we have only to ask and have; we
have 25*l.* a year besides all I mention: we have no trouble upon our
minds at the week's end how to pay for what we had.

Sidney's Emigrant's Journal, 1848

*As well as being a constant domestic preoccupation, food was an
easily accessible source of pleasure.*

I long to send you—indeed it is now on board—a great curiosity—
a rump of Cape beef, salted by the Fiscal. '*Oui, mi ledi, par mes
propres mains. Monsieur, les grands hommes sont égaux à tout.*' This,
with a mutton ham by Madame the Landdrost, will give you a
proper idea of our fare. If they are not good when they arrive it is no
fault of mine—I am *sure* they were good when they set off. I also
send you a box of ostrich eggs, the freshest I could obtain. I am told
by oiling them well and packing them with bran they often keep to
reach Holland good; if so, they may reach Wimbledon. There are six
eggs, one of them being emptied by me to make some cakes and to

try if it was good. Nothing could be more capital than my cakes; make your cook open one in the same manner, and if what it contains is sweet (which I hope it will be), then boil another to be quite hard, which is the way they are here reckoned most delicious, taken *whole* out of the shell and eaten with oil and vinegar; but be sure to have it served up entire, and not cut into pieces. If you will give one of the eggs to my sisters, and one to the Douglas's, or a share of one of them, I shall be much obliged to you. In the same box you will find a candle of my own making, of the vegetable wax (I have not burnt any yet, but I believe it burns dim, as its colour gives one a right to expect), and a small specimen of the syrup of the sugar tree; I could not make the box contain a quart, which I was sorry for. I forgot to put in a specimen of lead ore rough from one of the mountains; I'll enclose a scrap of it only to show you how pure it is found, in large pieces as great as your hand. I am sure there must be many wonderful things hidden in these stupendous hills.

> LADY ANNE BARNARD, *South Africa a Century Ago*,
> ed. W. H. Wilkins, 1901

Our dinner, at 6, was really so profuse, that it is worth describing. The first course was entirely of fish, excepting jerked hog, in the centre, which is the way of dressing it by the Maroons. There was also a black crab pepper-pot, for which I asked the receipt.—It is as follows; a capon stewed down, a large piece of beef and another of ham, also stewed to a jelly; then six dozen of land crabs, picked fine, with their eggs and fat, onions, peppers, ochra, sweet herbs, and other vegetables of the country, cut small; and this, well stewed, makes black crab pepper-pot.—The second course was of turtle, mutton, beef, turkey, goose, ducks, chickens, capons, ham, tongue, crab patties, &c. &c. &c.—Third course was composed of sweets and fruits of all kinds.—I was really sicker than usual, at seeing such a profusion of eatables, and rejoiced to get to my own room, and, after my usual levee of black and brown ladies, to go to bed.

> LADY MARIA NUGENT, *A Journal of a Voyage to . . .*
> *Jamaica*, 1839

We were seated on white mats, and welcomed by the chief people present. The feast was laid on a raised platform along the side of the room. There were a good many ornaments of the betel-nut palm, plaited into ingenious shapes standing about the table, so that I did not at first remark anything else. As we English folks could not eat fowl roasted in their feathers, nor cakes fried in cocoa-nut oil, they brought us fine joints of bamboo filled with pulut rice, which turns to a jelly in cooking and is fragrant with the scent of the young cane. I was just going to eat this delicacy when my eyes fell upon three human heads standing on a large dish, freshly killed and slightly smoked, with food and sirih leaves in their mouths. Had I known them when alive I must have recognized them, for they looked quite natural. I looked with alarm at Mab, lest she should see them too; then we made our retreat as soon as possible. But I dared say nothing. These Dyaks had killed our enemies, and were only following their own customs by rejoicing over their dead victims. But the fact seemed to part them from us by centuries of feeling—our disgust, and their complacency. Some of them told us that afterwards, when they brought home some of the children belonging to the slain, and treated them very kindly, wishing to adopt them as their own, they were annoyed at the little ones standing looking up at their parents' heads hanging from the roof, and crying all day, as if it were strange they should do so! Yet the Dyaks are very fond of children, and extremely indulgent to them.

HARRIETTE MCDOUGALL, *Sketches of Our Life at Sarawak*,
[1882]

Mrs McDougall was not alone in experiencing a close relationship with the 'locals'.

For ten days I sat making suits for [the porters] out of Indian calico, at the rate of three suits a day, so that each man might have a jacket and a pair of knickers . . . On the morning appointed for the departure, one hundred and twenty-five stalwarts . . . appeared, each with a supply of grain in a goatskin satchel sufficient to last for the outward journey . . . The nude warriors donned their [suits], in which none of them seemed to feel quite at home, and then all were ready for the march.

RACHEL WATT in *Memories of Kenya*, ed. Arnold Curtis, 1986

Sunday, February 7 1864. My poor Shaikh Yussuf is in great distress about his brother, also a young Shaikh (*i.e.*, one learned in theology and competent to preach in the mosque). Shaikh Mohammed is come home from studying in el-Azhar at Cairo—I fear to die. I went with Shaikh Yussuf, at his desire, to see if I could help him, and found him gasping for breath and very, very ill. I gave him a little soothing medicine, and put mustard plasters on him, and as it relieved him, I went again and repeated them. All the family and a lot of neighbours crowded in to look on. There he lay in a dark little den with bare mud walls, worse off, to our ideas, than any pauper; but these people do not feel the want of comforts, and one learns to think it quite natural to sit with perfect gentlemen in places inferior to our cattle-sheds. I pulled some blankets up against the wall, and put my arm behind Shaikh Mohammed's back to make him rest while the poultices were on him, whereupon he laid his green turban on my shoulder, and presently held up his delicate brown face for a kiss like an affectionate child. As I kissed him, a very pious old moollah said, '*Bismillah*' (In the name of God), with an approving nod, and Shaikh Mohammed's old father, a splendid old man in a green turban, thanked me with effusion, and prayed that my children might always find help and kindness.

I suppose if I confessed to kissing a 'dirty Arab' in a 'hovel' the English travellers would execrate me; but it shows how much there is in 'Mussulman bigotry, unconquerable hatred, etc.', for this family are Seyyids (descendents of the Prophet) and very pious. Shaikh Yussuf does not even smoke, and he preaches on Fridays. You would love these Saidis [Upper Egyptians], they are such thorough gentlemen.

LADY LUCIE DUFF GORDON, *Letters from Egypt*, 1865

I have passed nearly a week in a slight fever; shivering and hot. I was attended by a doctor of the country, who seems the most harmless creature imaginable. Every day he felt my pulse, and gave me some little innocent mixture. But what he especially gave me was a lesson in polite conversation. Every day we had the following dialogue, as he rose to take leave:

'Madam!' (this by the bedside) 'I am at your service.'

'Many thanks, sir.'

'Madam!' (this at the foot of the bed) 'know me for your most humble servant.'

'Good morning, sir.'

'Madam!' (here he stopped beside a table) 'I kiss your feet.'

'Sir, I kiss your hand.'

'Madam!' (this near the door) 'my poor house, and all in it, myself though useless, all I have, is yours.'

'Many thanks, sir.'

He turns round and opens the door, again turning round as he does so.

'Adieu, madam! your servant.'

'Adieu, sir.'

He goes out, partly reopens the door, and puts in his head—

'Good morning, madam!'

FRANCES CALDERON DE LA BARCA, *Life in Mexico*, 1843

The crew said the captain, a Scotchman, was so kind and let them have anything they wanted. He had his wife and little boy on board; she had been ill. The ship was becalmed, and we hoped the other islanders would go out to her, but they didn't seem inclined to do so. Later in the afternoon we heard to our surprise that they were going. We were so glad because of the letters. The captain sent us a whole heap of magazines and papers. We sent some young lettuces, and I only regretted we had not some flowers to send to his wife. The men did not return till the early hours of the morning. The captain sent us a bottle of lime-juice and would not take any payment for the groceries Repetto asked for. We feel much the invariable kindness of all the captains. The first boat's crew enjoyed themselves immensely on board. The captain played and sang to them. To add to his kindness he sent us a letter containing all the latest news; the first item of which was 'King Teddy going strong.'

K. M. BARROW, *Three Years in Tristan da Cunha*, 1910

There were certain delights inherent in the landscape (animal, vegetable, or mineral)—even in the bleak North Sea island of Helgoland:

Most of the lodging-houses were shut in winter and great fishing boats were drawn into the middle of the principal streets, high above high-water mark. There was nothing much to do in Helgoland at this season, except to look at the sea . . . but the air was so magnificent, and the climate so healthy altogether, that it made life, though very monotonous, still worth living.

FANNY BARKLY, *From the Tropics to the North Sea*, c.1898

November 7, 1891. At present Fanny [her daughter-in-law] is planting out cacao, mango, and breadfruit seeds; the first are a terrible bother, but she has now three hundred ready to be put into the ground. Each seed, I must tell you, must first be rolled in ashes to destroy insects, and then planted in a little basket made of plaited coconut leaves; these baskets are kept on the verandah till the 'shoots' appear, and then, basket and all, they are put in their permanent places, and the coconut leaf rots away in the earth as the roots enlarge and strike downwards. It entails a lot of labour, but should repay her, we hope, in the end. The oranges are at present in perfection, very juicy and sweet; and now that they are looked after, we can count on having them, as well as coconuts and bananas, throughout the year. Just now we are also rejoicing in unlimited pineapples, mangoes, and berbedines, the latter being very delicious and quite the South Sea equivalent—though I won't say equal—to strawberries at home.

MARGARET STEVENSON, *Letters from Samoa*, 1906

No venomous or hurtful animals are to be met with throughout the island; even the thick jungle which in India would be the hiding place of the savage tiger, is at the Mauritius only the retreat of the timid hare, and its silence, instead of being interrupted by the hissing of serpents, is disturbed only by the soft cooings of the dove.

LADY ALFRED BARTRAM, *Mauritius*, 1830

I had been warned before I went in of terrific hardships, of hunger, thirst, perpetual fatigue, sickness which hardly could be avoided, and dangers resulting from an undisciplined society, in which it was necessary not only to carry a revolver, but to be prepared on occasion to 'shoot quick.' I found none of these things. There was neither starvation nor brutality. Travelling quite alone, walking as other people walked—fifteen or twenty miles a day—over trails which, but for the passing prospector, were the exclusive haunts of wild animals and birds, I had not been three days in the country before I realised that a revolver was about as likely to be useful as it would be in Piccadilly. In the presence of untamed nature all humanity is friendly.

FLORA SHAW, *Klondike* [a lecture], 1899

I must now tell you a little about a Cape expedition of mine. Having been told that no woman had ever been on the top of the Table Mountain (this was not literally true, one or two having been there), and being unable to get any account of it from the inhabitants of this town, all of whom wished it to be considered as next to an impossible matter to get to the top of it . . . there was some ambition as a motive for climbing, as well as curiosity. And as Mr Barrow is just one of the pleasantest, best-informed, and most eager-minded young men in the world about everything curious or worth attention, I paid him my addresses and persuaded him to mount the mountain along with me. We were joined in the plan by two of my ship-mates, officers, and my maid chose to be of the party. I had a couple of servants, and a couple of boxes with cold meat and wine. Mr Barrow and I slung round our shoulders tin cases for plants, of which we were told we should get great variety on the top of the mountain. It is 3,500 feet in height, and reckoned about three miles to the top of it from the beginning of the great ascent, the road being (or rather the conjectured path, for there is no road) necessarily squinted in the zigzag way which much increases the measurement of the walk. At eight o'clock in the morning Mr Barrow and I, with our followers, set off. We reached the foot of the mountain on horseback, and dismounted when we could ride no more—indeed, nothing but a human creature or an antelope could ascend such a path . . . On the top of the mountain there was nothing of that luxuriancy of verdure and foliage, flower or herbage, described by travellers; there were roots and some flowers, and a beautiful heath on the edge of the rocks, but the soil was cold, swampy, and mossy, covered in general with half an inch of water, rushes growing in it, and sprinkled all over with little white pebbles, some dozens of which I gathered to make Table Mountain earrings for my fair European friends. We now produced our cold meat, our port, Madeira, and Cape wine, and we made a splendid and happy dinner after our fatigues. When it was over I proposed a song to be sung in full chorus not doubting that all the hills around would join us—'God save the King'.

'God save great George our King,' roared I and my troop. 'God save—God save—God save—God save—God save—God save— God save—God save—great George our King—great George our King—great George—great George—great George—' repeated the loyal mountains. 'The impression is very fine,' said Mr Barrow, with his eyes glistening. I could not say 'Yes,' because I felt more than I chose to trust my voice with, just then, but I wished 'great George our King' to have stood beside me at the moment, and to have thrown his eye over his new colony, which we were thus (his humble viceroys) taking possession of in his name.

LADY ANNE BARNARD, South Africa a Century Ago,
ed. W. H. Wilkins, 1901

Petersburgh, 1735. Dear Madam. You are too inquisitive and fond of odd things, for me to hope for pardon, if I should not tell you of a new diversion we have had at court this winter. There is a machine made of boards, that goes from the upper story down to the yard; it is broad enough for a coach, with a little ledge on each side. This had water flung upon it, which soon froze, and then more was flung, 'till it was covered with ice of considerable thickness. The ladies and gentlemen of the court sit on sledges, and they are set going at the top, and fly down to the bottom; for the motion is so very swift, that nothing but flying is a proper term. Sometimes, if these sledges meet with any resistance, the person in them tumbles head over heels; that, I suppose, is the joke . . . I was terrified out of my wits for fear of being obliged to go down this shocking place, for I had not only the dread of breaking my neck, but of being exposed to indecency too frightful to think on without horror . . .

ANON. [MRS VIGOR], *Letters from a Lady . . . in Russia*, 1775

The amusements on offer in New Zealand and Hong Kong were more orthodox, and, although mostly aimed at men, occasionally adaptable.

> Acclimatization Society.
> Agricultural and Pastoral Association.
> Benevolent Aid Society.
> Bible Society (Canterbury Auxiliary).
> Boating Club.
> Canterbury Chamber of Commerce.
> Club, Gentleman's, Christchurch.
> Colonists' Society, Lyttelton.
> Chess Club.
> Cricket Clubs.
> Debating Clubs.
> Female Home.
> Fire Brigade.
> Foresters.
> Freemasonry.
> Football Club, Christchurch.

Gymnasium Association.
Horticultural Society.
House of Refuge for Females.
Jockey Club.
Literary Society.
Musical Society, Lyttelton.
Orphan Asylum, Christchurch.
Railway Rowing Club.
Total Abstinence Society.

from *Southern Provinces Almanack* [New Zealand], 1866

My dear, I had nearly forgotten to tell you one thing: I've got the golf fever. There is a very fine links here with at least one natural bunker. This year, for the first time in the history of Hongkong, the Members of the Royal Hongkong Golf Club have most kindly and generously allowed us poor downtrodden women one afternoon in the week—Thursday to wit, a day on which they can't get off early themselves on the links because of its being so near to mail day. On this day, we are allowed, not only to play round the course, but even to come inside the sacred enclosure of the Club House railings and drink a cup of tea. Before this magnanimous rule was made, we had to drink our tea standing outside the fence.

'BETTY', *Intercepted Letters from Hongkong*, 1905

And then, of course, there was romance.

Father has gone again, and will remain until the home is finished. Then we are to go. *That* Mr Sanford . . . took a load of sash and flooring, and I've had a face to face encounter with him. I have heretofore only admired him from across the street, as he stops over there. They will camp out on the trip. Mr Sanford was to furnish the coffee, and asked father to have it prepared for him at the house, and he would call for it. We all 'had a finger in the pie.' Nan browned it, D[ora] ground it, and I made the bag to put it in.

There was a dispute as to who was to receive him, and deliver it. I quietly stationed Ada at the portholes, next the street, and when she saw him start over, she gave me the signal. So, duly equipped with the bag, after a vigorous scuffle, I stood by the door until he rapped. I opened it, and while I was accounting the cost of it, and he was fumbling in his pocket for a quarter to pay for it, mischievous Nan, who was on the floor behind the door, gave me a vigorous pinch on the leg, at which I screeched and before I thought shut the door in his face. Before I could open it, and apologize, he had gone. O, mercy! . . .

O! well, if I go to the country I will probably never see him again and I don't care if I don't.

MOLLIE DORSEY SANFORD, *The Journal . . . 1857–66*, 1976

We were made glad and happy yesterday by the arrival of our dear grandparents, and sweet cousin Mary. There were hardly expected yet, and no one was in town to meet them, but providence (Grandma says) sent them to Mr Sanford, who immediately stopped his work and came to pilot them through to this place. The dear old people had made the trip by land from Ind[ianapolis] in their own conveyance, which was an undertaking for a man over 70 years of age. They had made the trip without accident of any kind, until within a few miles of our place the dear old gentleman fell from the wagon and sprained his ankle, and but for By[ron] would probably have been killed . . . Grandma has taken it into her dear old head that he is my lover, and—I guess—well . . . *I* could make a confession here—I believe he is myself . . . We girls and he sat in the empty covered wagon until midnight last night talking and singing, and some way he found my hand and held it long and tenderly.

Ibid.

I was not in love with my husband when I married him. Of course I knew that he was a good man, and I respected him.

But polygamy is very hard on both the men and the women. It is hard on the first wife, and it is hard on the others also. My married life is like twenty years lost right out of my life. I do not like to talk about it, or even think about it. I would never want my children to know the heartbreak that I went through.

I had six children, three of them born while I was on the underground, during the polygamy raids. When we were on the underground, we would go to different places to the homes of our friends for a month or two at a time, till the deputies got on our trail, and then we would move on again. I stayed a while in Cottonwood, a while in Taylorsville and in other nearby settlements. I was a milliner and a dressmaker, and I could give lessons on the guitar, so I was always welcome wherever I went because I could be useful and more than earn my keep. My husband visited me, and we had our children in spite of the U.S. government. Irma and LaMont were born during the time I was on the underground.

I was just arrested once, and was brought before Critchlow and Verrian. They had our neighbors up there, and also my husband, and they asked us hundreds of questions. The deputy who came to arrest me, came in the early morning, just as I was getting breakfast. We were in our home, then, Irma was the baby, one year old, but she was large and plump, and I told him she was three years old, which was the legal limit. He held her on his knee and sat down and ate breakfast with us, and fed Irma her oatmeal.

I said, 'Do you think it is fair that we should walk all the way across the plains and build up a community and suffer hardships and make everything easy for your Gentiles to walk in, and then you should come and persecute us and follow us out to this place that you didn't want until we built it up?'

'Well,' he said, 'I've never thought of it that way. My brother-in-law is the marshall, and I was out of work, and he said to me, if you want to go out and arrest people I can give you a job. So that's how I happen to be arresting people.'

The judge asked me when I had last seen my husband and I said I couldn't remember. He asked the neighbors when they had seen him coming into my house, and they said they never saw him at all.

He asked me why I couldn't remember, and I said I have lived so many places it was impossible for me to remember. He asked how old my baby was and I told him three years. He asked a great many impudent and personal questions, and I always told him I couldn't remember. I could remember very well, but I just figured it was none of his business.

Finally he said, 'I know damn well you're lying, but I can't make out a case against you, so I'm going to let you go.'

ALMA E. M. FELT, *Memoirs*, *c*.1920

[T]he Women that go over into this Province as Servants, have the best luck here as in any place of the World besides; for they are no sooner on shoar, but are courted up into a Copulative Matrimony, which some of them (for aught I know) had they not come to such a Market with their Virginity, might have kept it by them untill it had been mouldy.

GEORGE ALSOP, *A Character of the Province of Maryland*, 1666

I began this in October, and it is now the 14th November; you will naturally wonder what has prevented my finishing it; I am going to tell you . . .

Here I have a little family history to relate. You must understand that I was in expectation of a little stranger, whom I thought might arrive about the end of December or the beginning of January; expecting to return to civilisation, I had not thought of preparing anything for him, when, lo! and behold, on the 4th November, at twenty minutes past four P.M., he made his appearance. The young doctor here said he would not live more than seven days, but, thank Heaven, he is still alive and well. He is small, but very much improved since his birth. I shall let him get a little bigger before I describe him. He is to be called Alatau, as he was born at the foot of this mountain range; and his second name Tamchiboulac, this being a dropping-spring, close to which he was called into existence. The doctor says the premature birth was caused by excessive exercise on horseback . . .

The day after my little man was born I got up, and, after walking about the room and doing a few odd things, I went to bed again, but the day after I got up after breakfast, and have been up during the whole day ever since.

MRS ATKINSON, *Recollections of Tartar Steppes*, 1863

Baby Edward was a year old on September 21st, and he was the Tristan baby, their baby, as well as ours, so they were determined to make his first birthday very special. Two days before, all the sheep were turned home from the Bluff, and eight of the largest were killed . . . Four of these were given by his godparents, and one and another provided potatoes and milk. Celebrations began early on September 21st. At 2.30 a.m. the bells were rung, and at 3.30 the baby was saluted by guns being fired outside the Parsonage, and by 4 a.m., or daylight, every house that could find one had hoisted a flag over the roof. At eleven o'clock a Thanksgiving Service in the church was held and well attended.

The cooks were kept very busy; the women made over forty puddings, and each family undertook to boil one or two, and, there not being enough saucepans on the island, they had to boil many of them in big tins.

The menu was stuffed roast mutton, plain roast mutton, boiled and baked potatoes, plum pudding, boiled suet pudding, potato pudding, jam tart with cream and sugar. Everyone was given tea after dinner, and when the cooks had washed up Mrs Repetto and I divided all the remains of the feast for the people to take home for their suppers. Before they left, everyone came and shook hands again, and said, 'Thank you, ma'am, for your good dinner.' This struck me as rather comical, as they had provided it all themselves, keeping flour, sugar, etc., from the *Dublin* stores for the occasion, but it certainly showed very good feeling. Edward received a most wonderful lot of things, very unique and characteristic of Tristan: over one hundred hen's eggs, twenty goose eggs, all kinds of socks and fancy mats, several frocks and bonnets, petticoats, three pairs of ox horns nicely polished, two pairs of mocassins, sea-shells, a coloured silk handkerchief, butter and milk, a silver-plated teapot,

a tablecloth and a silver chain, and some medals and brooches.
Each visitor went through the Tristan custom of giving the baby 'a
kiss and a slap.' You have a slap for each year of your life to make
you good, and a kiss to make you happy.

ROSE ANNIE ROGERS, *The Lonely Island* [Tristan da Cunha],
1926

EIGHT

DANGER AND
DESPERATION

There are no English families in Rangoon, and there is not a female in
all Burmah with whom I can converse.
Ann Judson, *An Account of the American Baptist Mission to the*
Burman Empire, 1827

Poor *Mrs Judson: there was nothing she could do but endure*
the loneliness. For some women—like the lady from whom
you will hear first—the whole business of being an emigrant
involved endurance. Being away from home was a bloody
nuisance from start to (longed-for) finish, and the best way to
get through it was to close the eyes, grit the teeth, lie back, and
think of England. But for most of the writers I have come across
there were highlights (the triumphs and delights . . .)—and defi-
nite low spots too.

Danger could come from any quarter. One woman describes
enjoying a quiet chat in the dusk on her verandah one moment,
while the next being catapulted on to the heaving ground by an
earthquake. Another, working entirely alone, became trapped by
a tree she was trying to fell as darkness—and the snow—closed
in. Here are accidents and illnesses, and irritations ranging from
rats in bed to disengaged toenails: all must be endured.

Those are just the physical problems, to which any emigrant is
liable. What marks out so many of the women's accounts,
though, is the emotional desperation they feel in certain situa-
tions. Especially those involving their children. One of the
reasons for Mrs Judson's resounding loneliness in Burma was the

loss of her only child, and some heartbreaking stories follow which could only have been written by mothers.

Another slightly oblique vulnerability suffered by women abroad—particularly British women abroad in the British Empire—is what I call the 'angel of Albion' syndrome. Angels of Albion were symbols (whose significance depended on one's viewpoint): they were flowers of British womanhood planted abroad to flourish and spread—and perhaps strangle whatever grew there already. Their being where they were, busily creating homes from home, was the most visible and practical evidence of colonization—or persecution; to attack them, weak and accessible as they were, meant attacking the men who loved them and who sent them. Hence their suffering, witnessed here, at the hands of the Indian Mutineers, the aborigines of Australasia, the North American Indians, and other oppressed peoples around the Empire.

All that comes later. This chapter of danger and desperation begins, however, with something altogether milder: the martyrdom of Mrs Sarah Courage.

I have but a small opinion of Christmas as a time of jollity. I always think it a solemn, not a jolly time, especially when one thinks of the 'tender and loving faces; dear faces far away'.

There is nothing like a brisk walk for raising the spirits, so I started off up the hill, taking two of the dogs for company. The tussock was very wet but I marched on as if I had an object, as indeed I had—I wanted a few ferns to mix with the flowers for decorating our dinner table that evening. We always dined late on high days and holidays, or when Fred would be at home in time; and I always made it a rule to have flowers or ferns on the table. The three days of wet and wind had spoilt the best of the flowers for the time; however, exertion, like virtue, is its own reward, and I felt more cheerful for the walk.

When I came back Rose met me with baby (who could toddle now) and said that Master had been in and left word that he would be back at two o'clock, and we would ride out together to the beach. He had just returned from the cow; she was swollen enormously and they feared she was dying. I took charge of baby while

Rose went to her dinner. As it was Christmas Day they each had a pint bottle of beer given them. Todd drank his off before dinner, and his wife's he drank during dinner, the selfish animal, the result being that he assumed the 'glorious Apollo' style, singing at the top of his voice, with refreshing gaiety. 'The Jolly Young Waterman',—that 'he was always first oars with the fine city la-a-dies' and 'as a waterman ne'er was in want of a fare'. He evidently felt merry enough in the midst of the surrounding desolation . . .

We had a delightful ride that afternoon but found the cow was dead. We got home in time for dinner, and what a dinner! Todd had killed a fine large turkey for our Christmas dinner; he plucked it and left the cleaning of it to his wife, and she forgot to remove the crop.

When we sat down to dinner, we thought it smelt very strong; in fact, as Fred remarked, one could 'smell it a mile off'. It was beautifully cooked and looked most appetising, but we could not understand from whence proceeded the peculiar sour smell.

While Fred was talking and preparing to carve, he stuck the fork into the crop; there was an explosion as of an airgun and such an awful smell. I rushed outside, and Fred over to the kitchen to interview Mrs Todd, who gazed at him in an imbecile way, which provoked him beyond endurance. What he said I do not know. I walked away; I dislike and deprecate quarrels above everything.

I met Rose, who said she had opened every window and door and the room would soon be ready for us again; but there was nothing for dinner but the remains of a cold saddle of mutton from the day before, and of course the plum pudding, which was unusually good, and I made my dinner of it entirely. Fred was very angry, but he calmed down afterwards, for the best of men is better full than empty, and I have lived long enough to see that the way to most men's hearts is through their stomachs.

Then, later on, Todd waxed quarrelsome and said he would 'make an example of his wife some day for leavin' in that scenter-pint' (viz. 'crop') and finished by giving her what he called 'a slap on the head' (he had a hand the size of a shoulder of mutton). Then he smashed the kitchen window. Fred spoke to him again about abusing his wife, but he was inclined to be insolent, so Fred gave him a month's notice to quit; and so ended an unhappy Christmas Day.

SARAH COURAGE, *Lights and Shadows of Colonial Life*,
[*c*.1896]

Oh dear, oh dear. Here is some real *trouble:*

Dunedin, 15 May [1878]
It is true that Catherine has been drinking but to nothing like the extent that Charlie made out. Well, something must be done . . . My letter is rather disjointed but you must excuse it for Catherine puts everything out of my head. It appears that a sergeant of the police telegraphed to Charlie, 'wife delirious, what is to be done?' Well, my word he has driven her to it for she says that she did not touch a drop for eight months after coming from Nelson but she found he was carrying on as bad as ever with Mrs Lyons and of course that drove her to desperation.

She has done her utmost by keeping the house nice to keep him right. And she was keeping the house on £3 a week thinking that Charlie was banking another three. But it is quite evident he did not do so for he has no money. Mr Spragg (a gentleman in the *Times* office who has been like a brother to Catherine, I really don't know what would have become of Catherine the last few weeks but for him), showed me a telegram which Charlie sent him the other day asking him to lend £5, which he did not do although he offered to lend to Catherine—at least he offered to pay the butcher or baker or anything like that to keep her going a bit . . .

My word we had a night of it last night. Catherine seems to be nearly at her wits end . . . She has been drinking rather freely I think . . .

Catherine seems to think that if Charlie . . . is really tired of her he ought to put all the children to a boarding school and she could then earn her own living . . .

PHOEBE LANGTON, *Letter*, 1878
[The original names have been changed to respect the family's wishes]

Ever watchful as I was, I noticed little changes in my husband, which under ordinary circumstances would have escaped my observation. By this time one all-absorbing idea had taken possession of my mind, and my husband's thoughts, I believe, were turned in the same direction—only our wishes did not exactly coincide. Polygamy was the thought common to both, but upon its desirability we entertained dissimilar views.

A man with Polgamy upon his mind was then a creature which I did not understand, and which I had not fully studied. Some years later, when I had a little more experience in Mormonism, I discovered several never-failing signs by which one might know when a man wished to take another wife. He would suddenly 'awaken to a sense of his duties;' he would have serious misgivings as to whether the Lord would pardon his neglect in not living up to his privileges; he would become very religious, and would attend to his meetings—his 'testimony meetings,' singing meetings, and all sort of other 'meetings,' which seemed just then to be very numerous, and in various other ways he would show his anxiety to live up to his religion. He would thus be frequently absent from home, which, of course, 'he deeply regrets', as 'he loves so dearly the society of his wife and children.'

One evening, when [my husband] came home, he seemed preoccupied, as if some matter of importance were troubling his mind. This set me thinking, too. I saw that he wanted to say something to me, and I waited patiently. 'I am going to the ball,' he presently remarked, 'and I am going alone, for Brother Brigham wishes me to meet him there.' I knew at once what was passing in his mind, and dared not question him. He went and saw Brigham. What passed between them I do not know; but, when my husband returned, he intimated to me that it had been arranged that he should take another wife.

The idea that some day another wife would be added to our household was ever present in my mind, but somehow, when the fact was placed before me in so many unmistakable words, my heart sank within me, and I shrank from the realization that *our* home was at last to be desecrated by the foul presence of Polygamy.

Almost fainting, now that the truth came home to me in all its startling reality, I asked my husband when he proposed to take his second wife.

'Immediately,' he replied; 'that is to say, as soon as I can.'

FANNY STENHOUSE, *An Englishwoman in Utah*, 1880

When I was about fourteen years old, I learned dressmaking. I worked for nothing as an apprentice to Mrs T. B. H. Stenhouse for six weeks. She wanted me to stay for six months, but I couldn't see the fun of working six months for nothing, and I decided to get out where I could get some money.

Mrs Stenhouse had her millinery and dressmaking shop on the east side of East Temple Street, between First and Second South. She was a French [Jersey] woman, very aristocratic and over-bearing in her manner. She was not attractive in appearance. She was light complected, and coarse looking, with a big round face. She was very excitable and very bossy, and things had to go her way, or she made a terrible fuss and there was the devil to pay. She was a good dressmaker, and a hard taskmaster. I learned a lot from her. She used to put a lot on me, when she found out that I had ability in cutting out, fitting and sewing. I had made my own clothes as a child, so I already knew something about sewing. I used to fit the bodices for her . . .

Mr Stenhouse was quite a fine looking man. As I remember him he had gray whiskers and slightly gray hair. He was tall, and stately looking, very refined, and very brilliant. He married Belinda Pratt for his second wife. She was the daughter of Parley P. Pratt, and was young and pretty. But Belinda soon left him, because Mrs Stenhouse put up such a terrible row . . .

Mr Stenhouse, along with many others, was very much in love with Zina Young. But she wouldn't even look at him. She knew that he was refined, and well educated, and brilliant, but she did not like his wife, and she knew what she would be stepping into if she went into that family!

ALMA E. M. FELT, *Memoirs*, c.1920

133

Worrying about the children, or watching them suffer, was described by one woman as the twist of the knife used by fate to wound such credulous emigrants as she.

A dreadful thing happened to me last night . . . I was sitting in a small inner room in the big hotel, only one other woman there, and I meant to be so brave, when into the room there rushed a boy, just like my own boy, the same age, the same height, with the same radiant joyous face, the same dear loving eyes. He came with arms outstretched, and calling 'Mother,' threw himself into the arms of the other woman, and covered her happy face with kisses.

Then something touched those elemental depths which, thank Heaven, are not often moved. A sense of the anguish of a thousand mothers, who pay for India with their babies, like birds dropped from the parent nest before their wings have learnt to fly, swept over a lonely woman, and there, in the sight of all that happiness, she wept.

One thing you must promise me. If you ever hear Anglo-Indian women called shallow and frivolous, if they ever seem to others to be vain pursuers of the empty bubble of an hour, will you remember there may be another side to the shield? I know that there is an alternative, to shirk no suffering, which brings with it understanding, the strength to endure, and that strange possession, peace. Only do not let any one be too hard on them. It may be cowardice, or it may be their own kind of courage, that makes them shut their ears to baby voices, or turn their eyes from haunting baby faces, to be resolutely gay.

ANNE WILSON, *Letters from India*, 1911

I do not think a residence on a slave plantation is likely to be peculiarly advantageous to a child like my oldest. I was observing her today among her swarthy worshippers, for they follow her as such, and saw, with dismay, the universal eagerness with which they sprang to obey her little gestures of command. She said something about a swing, and in less than five minutes headman Frank had erected it for her, and a dozen young slaves were ready to swing little 'missis'. [T]hink of learning to rule despotically your fellow creatures before the first lesson of self-government has been well spelled over! It makes me tremble; but I shall find a remedy, or remove myself and the child from this misery and ruin.

FRANCES BUTLER [KEMBLE], *Journal*, 1835

Before closing this letter, I have a mind to transcribe to you the entries for today recorded in a sort of daybook, where I put down very succinctly the number of people who visit me, their petitions and ailments, and also such special particulars concerning them as seem to me worth recording. You will see how miserable the physical condition of many of these poor creatures is; and their physical condition, it is insisted by those who uphold this evil system, is the only part of it which is prosperous, happy, and compares well with that of Northern laborers. Judge from the details I now send you; and never forget, while reading them, that the people on this plantation are well off, and consider themselves well off, in comparison with the slaves on some of the neighboring estates.

Fanny has had six children; all dead but one. She came to beg to have her work in the field lightened.

Nanny has had three children; two of them are dead. She came to implore that the rule of sending them into the field three weeks after their confinement might be altered.

Leah, Caesar's wife, has had six children; three are dead.

Sophy, Lewis's wife, came to beg for some old linen. She is suffering fearfully, has had ten children; five of them dead. The principal favor she asked was a piece of meat, which I gave her . . .

Charlotte, Renty's wife, had had two miscarriages, and was with child again. She was almost crippled with rheumatism, and showed me a pair of poor swollen knees that made my heart ache. I have promised her a pair of flannel trousers, which I must forthwith set about making.

Sarah, Stephen's wife; this woman's case and history were alike deplorable. She had had four miscarriages, had brought seven children into the world, five of whom were dead, and was again with child. She complained of dreadful pains in the back, and an internal tumor which swells with the exertion of working in the fields; probably, I think, she is ruptured. She told me she had once been mad and had run into the woods, where she contrived to elude discovery for some time, but was at last tracked and brought back, when she was tied up by the arms, and heavy logs fastened to her feet, and was severely flogged. After this she contrived to escape again, and lived for some time skulking in the woods, and she supposes mad, for when she was taken again she was entirely naked. She subsequently recovered from this derangement, and seems now just like all the other poor creatures who come to me for help and pity. I suppose her constant childbearing and hard labor in the fields at the same time may have produced the temporary insanity . . .

This is only the entry for today, in my diary, of the people's complaints and visits. Can you conceive a more wretched picture than that which it exhibits of the conditions under which these women live? Their cases are in no respect singular, and though they come with pitiful entreaties that I will help them with some alleviation of their pressing physical distresses, it seems to me marvelous with what desperate patience (I write it advisedly, patience of utter despair) they endure their sorrow-laden existence.

Ibid.

The 'angels of Albion' syndrome I mentioned in the introduction to this chapter victimized hundreds of women abroad in the more troubled territories of Empire.

[In Sitapoor] we lived a most happy life—for about four months. At first we stayed with [Commissioner] and Mrs Christian till our house was ready—such a nice little bungalow, with a big garden and our pets Uncle C[overley] mostly had given us—our Arab, and spotted deer, and gazelles, and spotted Barbary goats, and minahs, and chicaws [a sort of partridge] and green pigeons etc. etc., and white bullocks to irrigate the garden—and my brother had a buggy and horse and his Arab.

All this time rumours of disturbances were going on . . . Then in May, Meerut, I think, began, and we all got ready, though all the officers were quite certain *their* troops were faithful! However, everybody, civilians too, went about armed, and it was settled, should there be an outbreak, that all should go to the Christians' house. Mr C. tried to get elephants to send the ladies in to Lucknow on—unsuccessfully.

One morning—the 2nd June—we had just had prayers and were at breakfast when someone, Mr Christian, I think, came in to tell us another place [Shahjehanpur] had mutinied, and the native soldiers were marching on Sitapoor; that all ladies were to go to his house, and that the men were going to defend a bridge the mutineers must cross. A number of extra men had been enrolled and drilled—they turned out worse than the rest—and all our troops mutinied that day, 2nd June 1857, and against such heaps of natives what could our few English officers do! Mrs Christian's house was full of ladies and children. One poor fellow came in to have his wounds dressed—Mrs Christian's nurse[maid], looking ghastly herself, was doing it—then all the gentlemen rushed in, saying all the troops had turned against us (they had fought their way back to the house). Then the confusion was dreadful: people could not find their husbands—Mrs Christian was looking for hers, crying, my dear sister trying to comfort her . . . The house was all barricaded to keep out the natives, but fighting was useless: the natives were hacking down the barricades in front, and we all got out at the other side of the house in hope of hiding in the jungle . . .

Well, only half of a French window door could be got open and everybody was forcing their way out, regardless of anyone else. That was how we lost Georgie [her sister]. Mountstuart's hand I had got tight hold of—and kept, though my arm was nearly broken. Directly we were out, we ran across an open plain, towards the jungles, thinking my sister was with us. Then I noticed an extraordinary whistling noise everywhere and stopped: I had never been out like that . . . in the middle of the day before and thought it had something to do with the sun! [I] said 'what's that?' My brother quietly answered, 'the bullets'. Then I got frightened and said 'Oh, we mustn't stop here!' and rushed on with him, but after a second, stopped, noticing

Georgie was not with us. Looking back we saw her with Mrs Christian's English nurse, trying to quiet the baby and cover it from the sun: [it was] the last time I saw her, my poor sister . . .

Then we saw half a dozen men pursuing us, shooting now and then. Running as fast as we could, I ran into a thorny bush, and my white muslin dress was caught in tight. Poor M. threw himself on to the bush to tear it off me, and I could see all the colour leave his face as the thorns ran into him. We ran on and thought we had got away from our pursuers, when we saw them scuttling on the opposite side of a ravine. We got down into it to hide from their shots, and the last we saw of the poor Thornhills was him hiding his wife and child in a cleft, and standing in front of them. We heard afterwards that they were not killed there, but farther down the river.

We crossed through the river, calling them [the Thornhills] to follow us. I lost my shoes in it and fell on my face, and the pistol I had got wet. M. pulled me up: we had to climb a steep bank. The men saw us, yelled and fired—one shot was so close I looked to see if my arm was hurt and can almost feel the wind of it now—but we went on quite slowly—our running was over—and we thought the poor Thornhills must get killed where they were. We went through bushes and trees—one took my hat off and I did not take it again. A little further on, we sat down in a nook: no one was following us. I pulled off the muslin skirt which had been such a trouble as we sat, with our gun and pistol ready, listening.

I remember thinking how lovely the jungle was, and said to my brother I can't bear to be killed. M. said how could one bear to live, with such horror going on.

MADELINE JACKSON, *Reminiscences* [of 1857]

23 Mon   Like rain   did not wash   Mr & Mrs McKay were murdered at Reedy Creek Gulgong by the Blackfellows, the same ones that killed the Newberry family on Friday night. The police & civilians & Trackers after them, they are traveling fast.
24 Tues   Fine day. We washed. Retta went for violin lessons. I paid Mr Walshe 11/– for 6 lessons. The Blacks murdered Mrs O'Brien & child & wounded one other woman at Ulan and

Casselles on their way to Waller where they intend to kill more. They have killed eight altogether.

25 Wed   Terribly windy. Katie went down to Johnies in the morning One of the blacks, Jackie Underwood, was captured at Leadville all the police & Civilians after the other blacks. China War raging.

26 Thu   Cloudy like rain. Retta went down to Johnies to get our tea, 20 lbs at 1/6, from Griffiths Bros. I don't care for it. There are over 50 policemen & a lot of civilians & trackers after Jimmie & Joe Governor, the blackfellows & murderers. The Breelong murder which happened on the 20th inst. was the cruelest & worst murder that was ever committed in Australasia, there was four killed with tommighawks & two not expected to live.

27 Fri   Fine day. We heard that Pat Tierney of Waller was shot but fancy it's only a rumour. Kernin Fitzpatrick of Waller was shot dead by the blacks.

28 Sat   Beautiful day.

ELIZABETH TIERNEY, *Diary*, 1896–1909

I was fain to go and look after something to satisfie my hunger, and going among the Wigwams, I went into one, and there found a Squaw who shewed her self very kind to me, and gave me a piece of Bear. I put it into my pocket, and came home, but could not find an opportunity to broil it, for fear they would get it from me, and there it lay all that day and night in my stinking pocket. In the morning I went to the same Squaw, who had a Kettle of Ground nuts boyling; I asked her to let me boyle my piece of Bear in her Kettle, which she did, and gave me some Ground-nuts to eat with it: and I cannot but think how pleasant it was to me. I have some-time seen Bear baked very handsomly among the English, and some like it, but the thoughts that it was Bear, made me tremble: but now that was savoury to me that one would think was enough to turn the stomach of a bruit Creature.

One bitter cold day, I could find no room to sit down before the fire: I went out, and could not tell what to do, but I went in to another Wigwam, where they were also sitting round the fire, but the Squaw laid a skin for me, and bid me sit down, and gave me some Ground-nuts, and bade me come again: and told me they would buy me, if they were able, and yet these were strangers to me that I never saw before. . .

Soon afterwards:

We took up our packs and along we went, but a wearisome day I had of it. As we went along I saw an English-man stript naked, and lying dead upon the ground, but knew not who it was. Then we came to another Indian Town, where we stayed all night. In this Town there were four English Children, Captives; and one of them my own Sisters. I went to see how she did, and she was well, considering her Captive-condition. I would have tarried that night with her, but they that owned her would not suffer it. Then I went into another Wigwam, where they were boyling Corn and Beans, which was a lovely sight to see, but I could not get a taste thereof. Then I went to another Wigwam, where there were two of the English Children; the Squaw was boyling Horses feet, then she cut me off a little piece, and gave one of the English Children a piece also. Being very hungry I had quickly eat up mine, but the Child could not bite it, it was so tough and sinewy, but lay sucking, gnawing, chewing and slabbering of it in the mouth and hand, then I took it of the Child, and eat it my self, and savoury it was to my taste. Then I may say as Job, Chap. 6. 7. *The things that my soul refused to touch, are as my sorrowfull meat.* Thus the Lord made that pleasant refreshing, which another time would have been an abomination. Then I went home to my mistresses Wigwam; and they told me I disgraced my master with begging, and if I did so any more, they would knock me in head: I told them, they had as good knock me in head as starve me to death.

MARY ROWLANDSON, *The Soveraignty and Goodness of GOD . . . Being a Narrative of . . . Captivity and Restauration*, 1682

In the darkness of our ride I conceived a plan for the escape of little Mary. I whispered in her childish ear, 'Mary, we are only a few miles from our camp, and the stream we have crossed you can easily wade through . . . Drop gently down, and lie on the ground for a little while, to avoid being seen; then retrace your steps, and may God in mercy go with you. If I can, I will follow you.'

The child, whose judgement was remarkable for her age, readily acceded to this plan; her eye brightened and her young heart throbbed as she thought of its success.

Watching the opportunity, I dropped her gently, carefully, and unobserved, to the ground, and she lay there, while the Indians pursued their way, unconscious of their loss.

To portray my feelings upon this separation would be impossible. The agony I suffered was indescribable. I was firmly convinced that my course was wise—that I had given her the only chance to escape within my power; yet the terrible uncertainty of what her fate might be, was almost unbearable . . .

It must have been something more than a vague hope of liberty to be lost or won that guided the feeble steps of the child back on the trail to a bluff overlooking the road where, weary from the fatigue and terror of a night passed alone on the prairie, she sat, anxious but hopeful, awaiting the coming of friends. Rescue was seemingly near, now that she had reached the great road, and she knew that there would be a passing train of emigrants ere long.

It was in this situation that she was seen by some passing soldiers . . . They had been pursued by Indians the day before; had also passed the scene of the destruction of our trains; and believed the country swarming with Indians. Their apprehensions were, therefore, fully aroused, and, fearing the little figure upon the distant bluff might be a decoy, to lead them into ambush, hesitated to approach . . . However, they were about crossing to the relief of the little girl, when a party of Indians came in sight, and they became convinced it was a decoy, and turned and fled . . .

The agony that poor child endured as the soldiers turned away, and the war-whoop of the savage rang upon her terrified soul, is known only to God.

FANNY KELLY, *Narrative of My Captivity among the Sioux Indians*, 1873

Late one evening, about the 10th of January [1813], a friendly Indian came running to our house, in a great fright, and told Mr Reed that a band of the bad Snakes called the Dog-rib tribe, had burnt the first house that we had built, and were coming on whooping and singing the war-song . . . I took up my two children, got upon a horse, and set off to where my husband was trapping; but the night was dark, the road bad, and I lost my way. The next day being cold and stormy, I did not stir. On the third day, late in the evening, I got in sight of the hut, where my husband and the men were hunting; but just as I was approaching the place, I observed a man coming from the opposite side, and staggering as if unwell; I stopped where I was till he came to me. Le Clerc, wounded and faint from loss of blood, was the man. He told me that La Chapelle, Rezner, and my husband had been robbed and murdered that morning . . . [whereupon he too died.]

I was now at a loss what to do: the snow was deep, the weather cold, and we had nothing to eat. To undertake a long journey under such circumstances was inevitable death. Had I been alone I would have run all risks and proceeded; but the thought of my children perishing with hunger distracted me. At this moment a sad alternative crossed my mind: should I venture to the house among the dead to seek food for the living? I knew there was a good stock of fish there; but it might have been destroyed or carried off by the murderers; and besides, they might still be lurking about to see me; yet I thought of my children. Next morning, after a sleepless night, I wrapped my children in my robe, tied my horse in a thicket, and then went to a rising ground, that overlooked the house, to see if I could observe anything stirring about the place. I saw nothing.

Mrs Dorion managed to find some food amongst the bodies of her husband and his friends, before travelling on:

. . . 'till I and the horse could travel no more . . . I selected a lovely spot at the foot of a rocky precipice, in the Blue Mountains, intending there to spend the remainder of the winter. I killed my horse, and hung up the flesh on a tree for my winter food. I built a small hut with pine branches, long grass, and moss, and packed it

all round with snow to keep us warm, and this was a difficult task
... In this solitary dwelling I passed fifty-three lonely days.

MRS DORION in *Heroic Women of the West*, ed. John Frost,
1854

There would be precious little comfort in the climate and the
wilderness outside.

March 18, 1795. A person lately crossing Lake Champlain passed
a large Hole in the Ice and an infant alive lying by the side of it. By
tracks it appeared as if a Sleigh had fallen in and it was known that
a heavily-laden Sleigh with families in it left the country on the
opposite shore the day before, probably the Mother threw the
Child out as the Sleigh went down. The Gentleman carried the
Infant to Montreal where a subscription was raised for her
Maintenance—a good circumstance this, for the commencement of
a Heroine's life in a Novel.

ELIZABETH SIMCOE, *Diary . . . of Upper Canada 1792–6*,
ed. J. Ross Robertson, 1911

Our landlord apologised for some little mischance, by telling me
that his wife was away at the diamond fields. She had been thrown
out of the post-cart on her way up to them and had broken her leg
or her arm, I am not sure which. (This same individual actually
met with a similar accident on her return journey, and whichever
limb did not break going up she contrived to break coming down.)

HARRIET ROCHE, *On Trek in the Transvaal*, 1878

Now we are entering the realms of the picture-book pioneer:
indomitable, stoical, and infinitely capable.

We were making fine progress with our clearing and getting ready
to build a house in the spring. My brother and I worked early and

late, often going without our dinner, when the bread and meat which we brought with us was frozen so hard that our teeth could make no impression . . .

The last day of our chopping was colder than ever. The ground was covered by a deep snow which had crusted over hard enough to bear our weight . . . My brother had gone to the nearest settlement that day, leaving me to do the work alone.

As a storm was threatening, I toiled as long as I could see, and after twilight, felled a sizeable tree which in its descent lodged against another. Not liking to leave the job half finished, I mounted the almost prostrate trunk to cut away a limb and let it down . . . A few blows of my axe and the tree began to settle, but as I was about to descend, the fork split and the first joints of my left hand slid into the crack so that for the moment I could not extricate them. The pressure was not severe, and as I believed I could soon relieve myself by cutting away the remaining portion, I felt no alarm. But at the first blow of the axe which I held in my right hand, the trunk changed its position, rolling over and closing the split, with the whole force of its tough oaken fibers crushing my fingers like pipe stems; at the same time my body was dislodged from the trunk and I slid slowly down till I hung suspended with the points of my feet just brushing the snow.

The air was freezing and every moment growing colder; no prospect of any relief that night; the nearest house a mile away; no friends to feel alarmed at my absence, for my mother would suppose that I was safe with my brother, while the latter would suppose that I was by this time at home . . .

I prayed earnestly to God for forgiveness of my sins, and then calmly resigned myself to death, which I now believed to be inevitable. The pain had ceased, for the intense cold blunted my sense of feeling. A numbness stole over me, and I seemed to be falling into a trance, from which I was roused by a sound of bells . . . I screamed loud and long; the woods echoed my cries, but no voice replied. But the sound of my voice had broken the spell which cold and despair were fast throwing over me. A hundred devices ran swiftly through my mind and each device was dismissed as impracticable. The helve of the axe caught my eye, and in an instant by an association of ideas it flashed across me that in the pocket of my dress there was a small knife . . . I strove to cut away the wood that held my fingers in its terrible vice. In vain! The wood was like iron . . .

After a moment's pause, I adopted a last expedient. Nerving myself to the dreadful necessity, I disjointed my fingers and fell exhausted to the ground . . . I tore off a piece of my dress, bound up my fingers, and started for home.

HANNAH FOX in William Fowler's *Pioneer Women of America*, 1896

My trip into the interior was taken with Capt Abercrombi (the government expedition). We started Aug 5 with 24 wild horses each carrying from 200 to 400 lbs. It had rained for 41 days and was still raining when we started. About 5 miles—from Valdez to the foot of the glacier—was over rocks and creeks: first one horse would get away and then another; we had quite an excitement, as they did not take kindly to the pack.

We stopped to rest at the foot of the glacier for half an hour then started up over the big mountains of ice covered with rocks, the roughest road you ever saw: climbed up places you would never believe a horse could follow . . .

At times the fog was so thick we could not see ten feet ahead. Had two guides with us who kept getting lost. We had to travel 10 miles to make 2, back and forth . . .

We had to pack wood for a fire so as to make coffee, and such a time as they had! [E]verything was wet through: the mule that carried the wood had fallen in the lake: the men had to drag him out and his pack was soaked. After two hours we got our supper and didnt it taste good? Hot coffee, raw bacon and hard tack. You can believe me or not, but you could pour the coffee boiling hot into your cup and before you could get it to your mouth it would be almost cold. O, everyone was wet through. I wore my macinaw shirt and slicker, sou-wester and an extra pair of socks my macinaw blanket and rubber sheet. Got a sled someone had left here and made my bed by the fire. Well, I just thought I should freeze: the wind blew, and the rain and sleet were awful. The men had no blankets or anything so they just walked around to keep a little life in their bodies: two of them were packers on the Skaguay pass all last winter, and they said they never experienced such a night. At daylight, (3 A.M.) all were getting their breakfast—same as supper. The Capt. gave us each a hot drink at night and morning too. We left camp about 4 A.M. and had another day of it even worse than the first for we were getting higher up, it was growing colder and still raining. We had to go through about five miles of water and slush, and I was in it up to the knees sometimes. That was hard and cold. Talk about ice water—it is not in it with glacier water! My shoes were running water . . .

When I took off my socks my toe-nail was just hanging: I poked it back not wanting to pull it out for the glacier water had poisoned the toe and I did not want to be laid up; one of the soldiers was the same way; he could hardly step.

LILLIAN MOORE, *Reminiscences of the Klondike* [in 1898]

She is a tremendous sportsman and has shot a lion. She is all round extraordinarily clever and capable. Not only does she ride and shoot well, she knows goodness knows how many languages, has written grammars and vocabularies of some of these African dialects, helped her husband write two books, seems to have read and know most things, tames animals, or skins them when dead, paints, sings, I am told, and talks very well. So you may imagine she is interesting. I am afraid that is more than she finds me . . .

MRS MAURICE MARTINEAU in *Memories of Kenya*, ed. Arnold Curtis, 1986

Sept. 3d.—To-day our spirits were sadly damped by the hideous discovery of a very bad leak in the boat; and the prospect of being swamped, not to say devoured by wild beasts, sorely exercised all our faculties in devising some way of patching it together . . . If the leak suddenly became larger, all we could do was to make for the side and get out as much as we could of our provisions; but even then we should have been fortunate if we found a strip of ground firm enough to stand upon, for in these marshes that is not everywhere. There was no saying, too, how long we might not have to remain Robinson Crusoe fashion before any one came to our rescue, and then we could only expect to be picked up by a chance canoe. So we pressed together the edges of the steel plates which had come asunder, and tried to cement them first with bee's-wax, then with india-rubber, then with soft lard, and lastly, with gluten obtained by washing our arrowroot flour.

M. A. PRINGLE, *Towards the Mountains of the Moon*, 1884

A Plaster for Boils.—
Brown sugar, 1 teaspoonful.
Some yellow soap, scraped.
10 drops of laudanum.
Work with a soft knife into a paste, and spread a little on old linen with a heated knife.

This is an excellent plaster for bringing a boil to a head, and the laudanum soothes the pain . . .

Overdose of Laudanum, etc.—In case of an overdose of laudanum or opium or alcohol, immediately administer an emetic of mustard-and-water, and *above all keep the patient awake* and in motion, slapping him with wet towels and trotting him up and down the room till a doctor can be had.

HILDAGONDA J. DUCKITT, *Hilda's Diary of a Cape Householder*, 1902

An Englishman of very high rank in the Egyptian service wished to give a dinner party in his own house to the Prime Minister and various other Egyptian and English notables. He was a bachelor and did not often entertain, but he spoke to his servants and told them that he particularly wished the dinner to be a success. You can always count on your Egyptian, or rather Berberin servants, in any domestic crisis. They have a quick sense for the honour of 'our' house, as every good servant will say of his master's abode.

So the servants bestirred themselves and the guests sat down to an excellent dinner beautifully arranged. Good fish succeeded good soup, and then there was a pause. The host talked his best, but began to feel nervous. However, after a delay hardly long enough to attract the notice of the guests, the even procession of dishes recommenced and the evening was a great success. After the guests had departed the host said a word of praise to his head servant, and then remarked—

'By the way there was rather a long wait after the fish. Why was that?'

'May it please your Excellency the cook died of cholera.'

E. L. BUTCHER, *Egypt As We Knew It*, 1911

I have been confined to bed for a week with African fever. It commenced the day after Mr ——'s funeral, and the doctor had left the station for a little change. The first symptoms were an indescribably strange feeling in my head and eyes. The next day I was too ill to move; I could not lift up my head, and I had rheumatic pains all over my body. We had a small thermometer for taking the temperature with us, and by it discovered the amount of fever to be pretty considerable. We had understood that the fever we might expect in Africa would be of the intermittent kind, and that quinine should only be given in the cold stages; whereas, whatever my fever was, it certainly was not intermittent, and there were no cold stages. A—— was perfectly at a loss what to do, and many times nearly made up his mind to give me quinine; but as my temperature rose to 106° before the doctor came, he was afraid to risk it after the advice he had got. It was four days before the doctor returned. He was astonished to find my temperature so high, and at once administered large doses of quinine; and although very weak, the rapidity with which I recovered was marvellous.

One of the most disagreeable sensations in this African fever is the dreadful depression by which it is accompanied.

M. A. PRINGLE, *Towards the Mountains of the Moon*, 1884

The Seychelles, though generally so healthy, are occasionally
visited by an epidemic, which in these Islands takes a very virulent
form, such as measles or chicken-pox, and now began a terrible
time of misery for these lovely Islands. For seven months no one
was allowed to leave Port Victoria in a mail steamer. Scarcely any
ships would call there, so that provisions ran short, and famine was
added to the terror of the epidemic. Here was a British colony
dependent entirely for mails and transport upon a French
Steamboat Company, under the strictest quarantine regulations. A
British man-of-war came in with most of her crew ill with various
complaints, and among them, a case of what the Health Officer
took for some infectious disease, but which other doctors
pronounced to be virulent chicken-pox, while others again
declared it was small-pox, although some symptoms of the disease
were wanting. But whatever the malady was, it proved infectious
and fatal, for there were many deaths in the Islands . . .

[P]rovisions soon began to run out, all kinds of foods became
very scarce, there was no flour to be had, and rice soon rose to
famine prices, while meat became an unheard of luxury, as the
ships from Madagascar refused to touch; turtle also, was not to be
had, in fact, we were cut off from the world and from all supplies
entirely.

FANNY BARKLY, *From the Tropics to the North Sea*, [*c*.1898]

Different things annoy different people, of course.

I wish my box of gowns would ever arrive, don't you? I believe now,
if I see it when we go down from the hills this year I shall be lucky.
Do you recollect sending me a pink striped gown, a long time ago,
by a Mr R.? I had it made up only lately, and put it on new last
night: it was beautifully made, 'and I never looked more truly
lovely!' but there was an *odd rent* in the sleeve which, Wright said,
must be the tailor's fault. I put on my sash and heard an odd crack
under the arm; then Chance jumped into my lap, and there was an
odd crack in front. I sat down to dinner, and there was *another* odd
crack behind. In short, long before bed-time my dear gown was

149

what Mrs M. used to call 'all in *jommetry*'—there was hardly a strip wider than a ribbon, rather a pretty fashion, but perhaps too undefined and uncertain: that comes of being economical in dress.

EMILY EDEN, *Up The Country*, 1866

A mild kind of harmattan has been blowing for the last fortnight, which still causes the paper on which I write to curl up at the edges, as if it were held to the fire, and our most strongly-bound books to open their leaves of themselves.

ELIZABETH MELVILLE, *A Residence in Sierra Leone*, 1849

Yesterday, after dinner, Glennie having fallen into a sound sleep in his armchair by the fire-side, Mr Bennet and I, attracted by the fineness of the evening, took our seats to the veranda overlooking the bay; and, for the first time since my arrival in Chile, I saw it lighten. The lightening continued to play uninterruptedly over the Andes until after dark, when a delightful and calm moonlight night followed a quiet and moderately warm day. We returned reluctantly to the house on account of the invalid, and were sitting quietly conversing when, at a quarter past ten, the house received a violent shock, with a noise like the explosion of a mine; and Mr Bennet starting up, ran out, exclaiming 'An earthquake, an earthquake! For God's sake follow me!'

I, feeling more for Glennie than anything, and fearing the night air for him, sat still; he, looking at me to see what I would do, did the same; until, the vibration still increasing, the chimneys fell, and I saw the walls of the house open. Mr Bennet again cried from without, 'For God's sake come away from the house!' So we rose and went to the veranda, meaning, of course, to go by the steps, but the vibration increased with such violence, that hearing the fall of a wall behind us, we jumped down from the little platform to the ground; and were scarcely there, when the motion of the earth changed to a rolling like that of a ship at sea, so that it was with difficulty that Mr Bennet and I supported Glennie . . . Never shall

I forget the horrible sensation of that night. In all other convulsions of nature we feel or fancy that some exertion may be made to avert or mitigate danger; but from an earthquake there is neither shelter nor escape . . . Amid the noise of the destruction before and around us I heard the lowings of the cattle all the night through; and I heard too the screaming of the sea-fowl, which ceased not till morning. There was not a breath of air; yet the trees were so agitated that their topmost branches seemed on the point of touching the ground . . .

At four o'clock [a.m.] there was another violent shock; and the interval had been filled with a constant trembling, with now and then a sort of cross-motion, the general direction of the undulation being north and south. At a quarter past six o'clock there was another shock, which at another time would have been felt severely; since that hour, though, there has been a continued series of agitations, such as to shake and even spill water from a glass, and though the ground is still trembling under me, there has been nothing to alarm us. I write at four o'clock p.m.

MARIA GRAHAM, *Journal of a Residence in Chile*, 1824

Now that we are in a hut of our own, we are experiencing the novelty of housekeeping in the centre of Africa. Sometimes I wish our friends at home could have a peep at us. A few stout poles fixed in the ground, interlaced with branches and coated with mud, form our dwelling. All round it runs a verandah.

For the first few nights we were dreadfully troubled by rats. They ran along the ceiling and down the wall, and over us. At last we were obliged to keep a bamboo pole to knock them down; but now they are not nearly so bad, because whenever I saw one during the day, I used to call in some of the school-boys, and they had a great rat-hunt, ending by their invariably catching the unfortunate animal by the nape of the neck, just as a terrier would do at home. Having done that, they killed it by beating it with sticks, and finally cooked it for supper.

We have only a mud floor, and another great plague are minute house-ants. The legs of the table and the posts of the beds have all to be put into tins filled with water. Even these are not always successful in keeping them off; for unless they are emptied every day and filled with fresh water, the little creatures make bridges of their dead companions' bodies, and soon cover everything. Not very long ago, A—— laid down his sun-helmet, and did not notice that it was touching the wall. Shortly afterwards he put it on hastily to go out, but immediately the ants covered his head and ran down his face and neck in thousands. Although I felt very sorry for him, I could not help laughing, for it was such a curious sight, while he shouted 'Murder, murder!' They are particularly fond of our sponges, and sting most horribly, especially if they happen to get into our eyes. Once or twice they have even turned us out of bed. I am told that the natives have some ingenious plan of suspending their food from the ceiling, so as to prevent the ants from getting at it.

M. A. PRINGLE, *Towards the Mountains of the Moon*, 1884

I know of few things in this wicked world that have made me wish more often that polite society would accord the female sex a few expletives wherewith to let off the steam of its impatience, as the thin, steel-sharpening note of a curtain-imprisoned mosquito.

FLORENCE MARRYAT, *'Gup': Sketches of Anglo-Indian Life*, 1868

Miss Moore would not think a few paltry mosquitoes worth comment. We left her with her toenail hanging off in Alaska.

Arriving in camp I had a hot drink—went home and changed my clothes for dry ones, got my mail (I had about 20 letters waiting for me) read them all, went gadding, then laid down a few minutes but could not sleep,—got up and went to the hotel for my dinner and to a concert in the evening. Aside from a little stiffness I felt fine, not a bit tired, and up the next day as if nothing had happened.

LILLIAN MOORE, *Reminiscences of the Klondike* [in 1898]

As I said: everybody had to endure their emigrant life. It is the quality of that endurance that really counted; that made the difference between failure, and success.

NINE

STAYING ON

When I left England I was a blooming girl, now I am an old woman,
the mother of 12 children, grey-headed and almost toothless . . . I
forgot to tell you my age is 42 or 43.
G. Flower, *Errors of Emigrants*, 1841

If I were a prospective 'Jenny', like the fresh-faced, wholesome paragon with whom this anthology opened, I would not think such a future as Mrs Flower's much reward for my hard days' work as an emigrant wife. If I knew where to find them, I might be able to read more encouraging accounts, like those of the homesteader Elinore Pruitt Stewart and other like ladies quoted in this final chapter: they smack of independent spirits challenged and fulfilled in lands of comparative liberty and endless opportunity. Lives well worth staying on for, in fact—assuming one had the choice.

Most did not, and it probably took about 25 years to wear out the average emigrant woman. Because what all that cheerful and encouraging 'Jenny' literature did not mention was, that emigration for ordinary people was an investment of labour and life for which there would most likely be no return. No immediate return, anyway. Comfort and security in the colonies were too rare and dear to be bought by a single generation of immigrants. The best the founding families could do was plant the seed of establishment and prosperity, and then wear themselves out in the husbanding of it. Which is why this chapter is as much about leaving as staying on: there were thousands of British women during the span of this anthology who left far too soon in

*death, finished off by childbirth, overwork, loneliness, and the
neglect of a broken body, mind, or heart.*

*That was leaving by default; for those temporary emigrants
fortunate enough to leave by design, some bitter and some
relieved farewells are said, a few scathingly derisive of anyone
perverse enough to stay in the wilderness. It was probably ignorant people like this latter lot who gave the British abroad such
a bad name in some parts of the Empire: there follow here some
embarrassingly loud and priggish matrons who no doubt considered themselves sent out into a naughty world to teach it how to
behave. And what a lucky old world it was.*

The population of Hongkong as far as I am concerned consists of
William [her husband] and about three hundred more, none of
whom is Chinese.

'BETTY', *Intercepted Letters from Hongkong*, 1905

When I first saw the English residents in Madras turn out for their
evening drive, I mentally divided them into two classes—roast and
boiled—for all those who were not as white as dough were as red as
fire. When I reached Bangalore, however, I had to change my clas-
sifications. The treacherous climate of that place bears one advantage in its cutting winds and heavy dews; it freshens up the women
for a few months in the year, and when I saw them first in
September, they were looking their best, and continued to do so
until the following January.

I had not studied them long, however, before, putting their looks
on one side, I found they might be characteristically divided into
three classes—the gay; the religious; and the inane; and I deduced
that the latter were the only ones who were really too stupid to care
whether they lived in England or in India. For the other two
carried certain unmistakable signs about them that a life (whoever
it may be spent with) passed in exile from all the dear associations
of our youth, is so fraught at every turn with painful recollections,
that the heart that feels keenly must find something of more

engrossing interest than the routine of daily life, if it would bear up at all against the assaults of memory . . .

There are excuses in the fact that where a pretty woman has one temptation to be thoughtless in England she has fifty in India; that she is compelled by the climate to lead a life of so much idleness that any excitement comes to her as a relief; and that in many cases she is left alone and unprotected for months and even years, whilst her husband is away on foreign service, and she has not one of her own family, or his, to go to during his absence. Added to which, in England a gentleman has to obtain permission before he can call upon a lady; in India he may call on whom he pleases.

FLORENCE MARRYAT, *'Gup': Sketches of Anglo-Indian Life*, 1868

In India it is one of the conspicuous facts of social life that everybody knows everybody else's affairs. Nothing that could affect the reputation of any member of the community ever passes unnoticed. No skeleton is ever permitted to rest in its cupboard. But, on the other hand, to counter-balance the healthy effect of the searching light of this publicity it must be admitted that there is a great laxity of that mainstay of all social morals and manners: public opinion . . .

This fact in itself is a temptation to many to test the stringency of some of the stricter customs and manners of society. But there is another and greater temptation . . . namely, *opportunity*. Everyone knows what a powerful part opportunity plays in the making of crime: it is a no less successful factor in the composition of scandals. There is no station in India where two people who wish to meet often may not have the opportunity of doing so every day, in the natural course of events . . .

In excuse for those to whom laxity, liberty, and opportunity form an overwhelming combination of forces to which they eventually succumb, it must be urged that they are without many of the safeguards which would serve to protect them elsewhere. Amongst these . . . is that very real and wholesome restraint which a household of English servants undoubtedly tends to impose upon the liberties of social intercourse among self-respecting people.

MRS L. C. RICKETTS, *English Society in India* in *Contemporary Review*, 1912

My own opinion is that if you want to love your neighbours you should not see them too often, not from any misanthropic fad, but simply because of the limitations of human nature. Even Arctic explorers, with all the adventures and hazards attending such enterprises, have found how necessary it was to isolate each member of the party in turn, if they were to retain their sense of proportion, and not end by applying the microscope to one another instead of the telescope.

MRS ROBERT MOSS KING, *The Diary of a Civilian's Wife*, 1884

Extremely sound advice, given some of the neighbours' behaviour.

This once numerous and powerful tribe of south-eastern natives [the Booandik of South Australia] is now represented by a miserable remnant, which will in a few years, with the other aborigine peoples of South Australia, have withered away before the new mode of life forced upon them by the advent of European colonists in their midst, assisted too often by the cruelties practised upon them by the early settlers.

MRS JAMES SMITH, *The Booandik Tribe*, 1880

The Indians are often made a prey of and cheated by the unprincipled settlers, who think it no crime to overreach a red-skin. One anecdote will fully illustrate this fact. A young squaw, who was near becoming a mother, stopped at a Smith-town settler's house to rest herself. The woman of the house, who was Irish, was peeling for dinner some large white turnips, which her husband had grown in their garden. The Indian had never seen a turnip before, and the appearance of the firm, white, juicy root gave her such a keen craving to taste it that she very earnestly begged for a small piece to eat. She had purchased at Peterborough a large stone-china bowl, of a very handsome pattern, the worth of which might be a half-dollar. If the poor squaw longed for the turnip, the value of which could scarcely reach a copper, the covetous European had fixed as longing a glance upon the china bowl, and she was determined to gratify her avaricious desire and obtain it on the most easy terms.

She told the squaw, with some disdain, that her man did not grow turnips to give away to 'Injuns', but she would sell her one. The squaw offered her four coppers, all the change she had about her. This the woman refused with contempt . . . nothing would satisfy her but the bowl. The Indian demurred; but opposition had only increased her craving for the turnip in a tenfold degree; and, after a short mental struggle the squaw gave up the bowl, and received in return *one turnip*! The daughter of this woman told me this anecdote of her mother as a very clever thing.

SUSANNA MOODIE, *Roughing it in the Bush*, 1852

I love the Blacks. Some of them were my playfellows when I was a child at Naraigin . . . Sometimes one speculates whether in the far ages there ever dwelt a white man-god among them who taught the people knowledge of some things good and evil, and delivered to them the marriage ordinances . . .

MRS CAMPBELL PRIDE, *My Australian Girlhood*, 1902

Not just any old 'man-god', you notice, but a white one . . .
Having tried the emigrant life, only a fortunate few could choose *to stay or leave. Most merely responded, with more or less enthusiasm, to the inevitable.*

It is quite customary of a morning to ask 'how many died last night?'. . . . I cannot imagine what kind of stuff I am made of, for though daily in the midst of so much sickness and so many deaths, I feel myself much better than when in England.

A. M. FALCONBRIDGE, *Two Voyages to Sierra Leone*, 1794

Boulaq, June 15 1869. Dearest Alick. Do not think of coming here. Indeed it would be almost too painful to me to part from you again; and as it is, I can patiently wait for the end among people who are kind and loving enough to be comfortable, without too much feeling of the pain of parting. The leaving Luxor was rather a distressing scene, as they did not think to see me again.

The kindness of all the people was really touching, from the Cadi who made ready my tomb among his own family, to the poorest fellaheen. Omar sends you his most heartfelt thanks, and begs that the boat may remain registered at the Consulate in your name for his use and benefit. The Prince has appointed him his own dragoman. But he is sad enough, poor fellow, all his prosperity does not console him for the loss of the 'mother he found in the world'. Mohammed at Luxor wept bitterly and said, 'poor I, my poor children, poor all the people', and kissed my hand passionately, and the people at Esneh, asked leave to touch me 'for a blessing', and everyone sent delicate bread, and their best butter, and vegetables and lambs. They are kinder than ever now that I can no longer be of any use to them.

If I live till September I will go up to Esneh, where the air is softest and I cough less. I would rather die among my own people in the Said than here . . .

Cairo, Helwan opposite Bedreshayn, July 9 1869. Dearest Alick. Don't make yourself unhappy and don't send out a nurse. Miss Mathews has come out excellent and I am nursed as well as possible. My two reises, Ramadan and Yussuf, are strong and tender, and Omar is as ever. I am too absorbed in mere bodily suffering to wish anyone else to witness it. The worst is I am so strong. I rehearsed my death two days ago and came back again after being a whole night insensible . . .

God bless you, my dearest of all loves. How sad that your Nile project was too late.

Kiss my darlings all . . . I don't write very well, I suppose, being worn out with want of sleep and incessant suffocation.

Forgive me all my faults toward you. I wish I had seen your dear face once more—but not now. I would not have you here now on any account.

LADY LUCIE DUFF GORDON, *Last Letters from Egypt*, 1875

[May 23, 1855] Remember [me] to all enquiring friends if I have not grown out of all their memories. They are all quite fresh in mine. It seems but yesterday I left home. I think trouble makes us cling more to home. Goodbye. God bless you.

MARGARET FULLER, *Diary* [her last words], 1855

I have stolen away to a much-loved spot, where I love to sit and pay the tribute of affection to my lost, darling child. It is a little enclosure of mango trees, in the centre of which is erected a small bamboo house, on a rising spot of ground, which looks down on the new made grave of our infant boy. Here I now sit; and, though all nature around wears a most romantic, delightful appearance, yet my heart is sad, and my tears frequently stop my pen. You my dear Mrs L., who are a mother, may imagine my sensations; but, if you have never lost a first-born, an only son, you cannot know my pain. Had you even buried your little boy, you are in a Christian country, surrounded by friends and relatives who could sooth your anguish, and direct your attention to other objects. But, behold us, solitary and alone, with this one source of recreation! Yet this is denied us—this must be removed, to show us that we need no other source of enjoyment but God himself.

ANN JUDSON, *An Account of the American Baptist Mission to the Burman Empire*, 1827

On the whole it was rather dismal work getting to . . . pack off to school for the first time a very dear and very small boy whom I had hitherto cherished exceedingly, and with whom I hated parting as I never hated anything before. I had to buy him a horrid little Eton suit, of which he was intensely proud, but in which he looked such an absurd grown-up little manikin that my heart ached for the sight of him in pinafores again. As a special treat he was allowed to sit up to dinner on the night before leaving for school, and as I watched him afterwards in a smoke-laden billiard room, his blue eyes heavy with sleep, his baby mouth set with determination to keep awake, his podgy little legs encased in long trousers, and his chubby little neck encased in a hideous stiff collar, I could hardly bear to look at him. What, I thought, are cannibals, and wild animals, and obscure diseases, compared to a sight like this? Why do people imagine that it requires extraordinary courage and forti-tude to face these unknown and unlikely dangers and accept as a matter of course the parting of a mother with her boy?

MRS HORACE TREMLETT, *With the Tin Gods*, 1915

At Auckland they are building another lunatic asylum, as the present one cannot contain the ever increasing demands. Sometimes there are as many as from fifteen to twenty in a week seeking admittance; but this is no surprise to those who know what Colonial life *really* is, and also the trying effect of the climate. The chief causes of this insanity are exposure to the sun, a sun that beats fiercely on the head of the poor land toiler and pedestrian as no English sun beats, frequently accompanied by a burning wind, which seems to dry up all the juices of the body, and produces a burning thirst which is maddening. Then a large number fill the asylums whose minds have given way from grief at the loss of property, and utter disappointment at finding themselves quite deceived and unfit to cope with the hardships of the life awaiting them, and also bitter regrets at the remembrance of good homes broken up where they might now be thriving, if they had not forsaken them, giving too easy an ear to hope's flattering tale, and come thousands of miles with the hopes of 'bettering themselves.'

Under these circumstances grief takes heavy hold of our poor emigrant, both male and female, and the mind gets quite unhinged; and the better the class from which they sprang at home the more they suffer, and the more hopeless their case.

'HOPEFUL', *'Taken In'; Being a Sketch of New Zealand Life*, 1887

What price 'Jennies' now?

July 21st.—For several weeks now we have had no milk or butter. Edward has been very ill all the week. I have been much worried and unable to go to church or school. All the children here suffer a great deal from the poor quality and short quantity of food, more especially when the winter months come on. My husband is looking very thin and worried, but the neighbours are very kind and the women help with cooking and washing, as baby cannot be left. The sea is very rough to-day, huge breakers crashing right up to the bank. Rather a terrible sight.

August 28th.—Very short of soap, and our last tin of coffee. I have been looking over the stores and only got scant consolation.

August 29th.—We have one family here which had practically nothing to eat for days, and I wanted to give them some of our food as there are young children, but was told rather gruffly 'they could feed their own family.' The people here are very proud and sensitive on some points, so I said no more.

September 7th.—Still worried over Baby Edward: he is not doing well—cannot get suitable meals. The people will be getting penguin eggs soon, which will relieve the food situation, but it would seem rather hard elsewhere to have to live mainly on penguin eggs. Potatoes are getting very short.

September 10th.—Many gone for eggs. A great avalanche of stones fell down the mountain last night, making a noise like thunder or big guns—very alarming, but nothing hurt luckily. Since we have been here so many stones and boulders have fallen that the island looks quite different.

November 7th.—The island boats have gone to Inaccessible

to-day for birds for food and to look for wood. Some of the men showed very nice feeling, saying 'Goodbye' to us, because they expect to be away some days, and a boat might come and take us off to the Cape in their absence. They 'thanked us for our kindness and wished us good luck.'

November 27th.—We always have tea and supper in one. To-day we had dinner, tea, and supper all in one, at five o'clock. The children of the island haunt any kitchen where a meal is preparing, and I do not blame them. The last six months has been the shortest time since the *Dublin* was here two years ago. The storm of wind and rain did so much harm to the potatoes this year.

December 18th.—Christmas is coming and we are all preparing to make the best of the rather hard times, according to the proverb that 'it is a poor heart which never rejoices.' We have had a busy week, numbers of anxious mothers and children trying to get the problem of 'new clothes for Christmas' solved. We felt very sorry for them all, and soon I had given away every spare piece of calico or print I possessed to make new frocks or cappies or renovate old ones. One little girl managed it by having a nice white tablecloth converted into a frock; another fell back on mother's best petticoat, and one lad had trousers from a white sheet, two more used a mackintosh and a yellow canvas mail sack. Really they are wonderful contrivers.

January 16, 1925.—Will the New Year bring a ship? Our time is very nearly up now. Food is very bad still. Our meals for most of the week have consisted of a few boiled potatoes with one small cup of butter, and about one pint of milk daily between the three of us.

ROSE ANNIE ROGERS, *The Lonely Island*, 1926

It is frequently said, though very unjustly, that this climate never kills the English ladies; and, indeed, it must be allowed, that women do not so often die of violent fevers as men, which is no wonder, as we live more temperately, and expose ourselves less in the heat of the day; and perhaps, the tenderness of our condition sometimes prevents the violence of the disorder, and occasions a lingering, instead of a sudden, death. But most English women labour under the oppression of weak nerves, slow fevers, and bile: the disorders I have mentioned, and the continual perspiration, soon destroys the roses on the cheeks of the young and beautiful, and gives them a pale yellow complexion.

MRS KINDERSLEY, *Letters . . .* , 1777

April 14, 1892. Two more of our friends here are 'going home'; *she* for ill health and *he* having got six months' leave to take care of her. That is one drawback here, that the society, such as it is, is always changing; one no sooner gets to like people than they go away, and with that in mind it is hard to make friends with those who replace them.

MARGARET STEVENSON, *Letters from Samoa*, 1906

A circumstance happened at the Mauritius whilst I was there that excited a good deal of interest: a young French lady, in the possession of affluence, beauty, health—all that the world calls desirable—suddenly put an end to her existence by drinking laudanum. No cause could be assigned for this act: she was married to a man who seemed passionately attached to her, and was the idol of her mother, with an extensive acquaintance who esteemed and admired her; yet she found life so insupportable, that she committed suicide. She had been educated with far greater care than the generality . . . and was considered superior in talents and acquirements. A Creole gentleman, speaking of her unhappy end, attributed it to her having too much intellectual cultivation. 'Elle avait la tête exalté,' he said, 'par une education trop soignée, et en voilà le résultat!'

LADY ALFRED BARTRAM, *Mauritius*, 1830

There are several complaints prevalent in Burmah, which appear to be almost peculiar to fresh comers, the most curious of which I have heard called, for lack of a more technical name, 'the Burmese Ennui.' It was more likely to attack women than men (on account, I conclude, of the want of occupation), and took the form of a settled melancholy, due partly to the monotonous temperature, which, if not diverted by change of scene and action, had been known to degenerate almost into a state of idiotcy. A lady was sent to England on this account whilst we were resident in Rangoon, who had arrived at such a pitch of 'ennui' that she would neither eat nor drink, but sat all day doing nothing, with the tears rolling almost insensibly down her cheeks.

FLORENCE MARRYAT, *'Gup': Sketches of Anglo-Indian Life*,
1868

When the post has come in, the excitement of the day is over for most people in Ootacamund . . .

Ibid.

Boredom was no problem for Susanna Moodie: her life as an emigrant pioneer was full. Too full. The book she wrote describing it was a cautionary tale:

If [it] should prove the means of deterring one family from sinking their property, and shipwrecking all their hopes, by going to reside in the backwoods of Canada, I shall consider myself amply repaid for revealing the secrets of the prison house, and feel that I have not toiled and suffered in the wilderness in vain.

SUSANNA MOODIE, *Roughing it in the Bush*, 1852

My relations, when I came home, were inclined to console me for all I had gone through, by saying, 'At any rate, you have gained experience.' But it seems to me that there are some experiences—such as being half-murdered, for instance—that one is just as well without.

In addition to all the other disagreeables of being buried alive in a place like Langat, one loses all one's old acquaintance and makes no new ones; so that when we at length awoke from our six years' nightmare, we found ourselves all but friendless, as well as all but penniless. In short, I do not recommend the Malay Native States service to anyone who cannot begin, as some have begun, at the top, by being Resident.

EMILY INNES, *The Chersonese with the Gilding Off*, 1885

I went into the Bush of Muskoka strong and healthy, full of life and energy, and fully enthusiastic as the youngest of our party. I left it with hopes completely crushed, and with my health so hopelessly shattered from hard work, unceasing anxiety and trouble of all kinds, that I am now a helpless invalid, entirely confined by the doctor's orders to my bed and sofa, with not the remotest chance of ever leaving them for a more active life during the remainder of my days on earth.

AN EMIGRANT LADY, *Letters from Muskoka*, 1878

We had now given the land of liberty two years' trial, and had endured nearly two years of ill health; we therefore most cordially agreed in our determination to leave those to enjoy its blessings, who prized them—for our own part we had had quite enough. Acting on this impulse, as soon as we were sufficiently convalescent, we proceeded to arrange our affairs for departure, and, as concerns America, the day on which we reflect with the greatest pleasure, is the day we left it.

MRS FELTON, *Life in America*, 1838

Enough of the negative. Here are some success stories:

I never did like to theorize, and so this year I set out to prove that a woman could ranch if she wanted to. We like to grow potatoes on new ground, that is, newly cleared land on which no crop has been grown. Few weeds grow on new land, so it makes less work. So I selected my potato-patch, and the man ploughed it, although I could have done that if Clyde would have let me. I cut the potatoes, Jerrine helped, and we dropped them in the rows. The man covered them, and that ends the man's part. By that time the garden ground was ready, so I planted the garden. I had almost an acre in vegetables. I irrigated and I cultivated it myself.

We had all the vegetables we could possibly use, and now Jerrine and I have put in our cellar full, and this is what we have: one large bin of potatoes (more than two tons), half a ton of carrots, a large bin of beets, one of turnips, one of onions, one of parsnips, and on the other side of the cellar we have more than one hundred heads of cabbage. I have experimented and found a kind of squash that can be raised here, and that the ripe ones keep well and make good pies; also that the young tender ones make splendid pickles, quite equal to cucumbers. I was glad to stumble on to that, because pickles are hard to manufacture when you have nothing to work with. Now I have plenty. They told me when I came that I could not even raise common beans, but I tried and succeeded. And also I raised lots of green tomatoes, and, as we like them preserved, I made them all up that way. Experimenting along another line, I found that I could make catchup, as delicious as that of tomatoes, of gooseberries. I made it exactly the same as I do the tomatoes and I am delighted. Gooseberries were very fine and very plentiful this year, so I put up a great many. I milked ten cows twice a day all summer; have sold enough butter to pay for a year's supply of flour and gasoline. We use a gasoline lamp. I have raised enough chickens to completely renew my flock, and all we wanted to eat, and have some fryers to go into the winter with. I have enough turkeys for all of our birthdays and holidays.

I raised a great many flowers and I worked several days in the field. In all I have told about I have had no help but Jerrine. Clyde's mother spends each summer with us, and she helped me with the cooking and the babies. Many of my neighbors did better than I did, although I know many town people would doubt my doing so much, but I did it. I have tried every kind of work this ranch affords, and I can do any of it. Of course I *am* extra strong, but those who try know that strength and knowledge come with doing. I just love to experiment, to work, and to prove out things, so that ranch life and 'roughing it' just suit me.

ELINORE PRUITT STEWART, *Letters of a Woman Homesteader*, 1914

I like the back Woods as this is call'd better than any place upon Earth—I came into the country from Choice and I am a thorough American in principle and practice—We live in the same Log Cabins which we built when we first came here 15 years ago—very humble in appearance but plaster'd and colour'd withinside with deep porches back and front good size'd rooms neat clean airy and cheerful—they stand on a fine meadow like a Park—Blue Grass up to door situated on a beautiful Prairie—good Wells and good Tanks—it is a lovely Country.

ELIZA JULIA FLOWER, *Letters of an English Gentlewoman*, ed. Janet R. Walker and Richard W. Burkhardt, 1991

British mothers of Canadian sons!—learn to feel for their country the same enthusiasm which fills your hearts when thinking of the glory of your own. Teach them to love Canada—to look upon her as the first, the happiest, the most independent country in the world! Exhort them to be worthy of her—to have faith in her present prosperity, in her future greatness, and to devote all their talents, when they themselves are men, to accomplish this noble object. Make your children proud of the land of their birth, the land which has given them bread—the land in which you have found an altar and a home; do this, and you will soon cease to lament your separation from the mother country, and the loss of those luxuries which you could not, in honour to yourself, enjoy; you will soon learn to love Canada as I now love it, who once viewed it with a hatred so intense that I longed to die . . .

SUSANNA MOODIE, *Life in the Clearings*, 1853

Any woman who can stand her own company, can see the beauty of the sunset, loves growing things, and is willing to put in as much time at careful labor as she does over the washtub, will certainly succeed; will have independence, plenty to eat all the time, and a home of her own in the end.

From SANDRA MYRES (ed.), *Westering Women*, 1982

It is astonishing that most of the clatter concerning distressed women and distressful men comes not from the Colonies, where women are supposed to have got rid of the curb and ride on the snaffle, but from the wisest yet the shallowest and most provincial of towns, even London. The vacuity of the average London draw-ing-room is enormous, its real ignorance so vivid that it is pungent. The truth is, in the British Colonies, women have shared in the civic and national progress. They have seen cities grow up with their children; they have watched the cow-path turn into a side-walk, the side-walk to a pavement, the clap-board house to a mansion . . . They influence; they do not potter, and theorise, and play at being man. For real womanliness—primitive womanli-ness—there is still 'the Colonial' left.

MRS E. COLQUHOUN, *Women in the Colonies*, 1903

But not for everyone.

We must steadily set our faces against a further influx of delicate or unprincipled emigrants, who under the respected banner of domestic services are able to flout at philanthropists and employ-ers . . . [T]o enumerate a few of the bad results likely to accrue to the colony from a continuation of the present state of affairs:

(1) The certainty of many of these delicate women marrying in the colony and becoming the mothers of equally delicate chil-dren.

(2) The demoralizing effect in our young men of an influx of volatile and undisciplined young women of a low class.

(3) The terrible example to our children.
(4) The belittling in the eyes of our girls of the profession of domestic service.
(5) The desecration of our homes.

We cannot undo all the harm already done, but we can, if we will but rouse ourselves, prevent more harm being done us in the future. We can stand on the defensive and refuse to admit the landing on our shores of undesirables who but for our encouragement and assistance would never dream of coming.

MAY HELY HUTCHINSON, *Female Emigration to South Africa*, in *Nineteenth Century*, 1902

The Pioneer spirit is absolutely essential if you want to hold your own. There is work in plenty for the right sort of woman, but if anyone has a hankering for the fleshpots of Egypt, let them stay in England.

[ANON. (a maternity nurse in Alberta), 1913] in *New Horizons: A Hundred Years of Women's Migration*, 1963

Throughout the official annals of female emigration (i.e. the politically correct publications with which this anthology began and will end), the moral influence of 'the right sort of woman' could never be underestimated. She did not even have to be a **real** *woman.*

I have begged them to have a lay figure of a lady, carefully draped, set up in their usual sitting room and always to behave before it as if it were their mother, or some other dignified lady. They did not quite promise this, but they seemed quite duly impressed with the neccessity of attending somewhat to those little trifles which are very often altogether neglected by young gentlemen at stations; which neglect by degrees tells upon their general habits, or even character, in a much stronger way than you might suppose.

CHARLOTTE GODLEY, *Letters from Early New Zealand*, 1936

She is never too over-burdened with care to meet her husband with a smile, and he gives a sigh of relief as he . . . takes off all business cares and settles himself down into the enjoyment of home and its comforts . . .

Her hair may gradually become silvered, and her face lined with wrinkles; her step grow less light and buoyant, and her smiles be more sad and wistful, but it will never become less sweet and pleasant to her dear home circle. To many her life may seem tame and monotonous, but she enjoys that purest of all earthly pleasures—that of promoting the happiness of others.

To the casual observer it may seem that her husband and children are not fully sensible of her worth; but the time *will* come when those loving eyes are closed for ever—when that tender heart has stilled its throbs—when that voice, upon whose tone was the law of kindness, is hushed—when the busy hands, never idle, never weary, are calmly folded over the breast which has been the resting-place of aching heads and sorrowing hearts—when the feet so swift to run shall run no more—and all that is left of the good house-mother is a green mound and a marble stone—except the memories ever verdant . . . in the hearts of her life's companion and her children . . . [S]he will be shrined in their souls' core, as the embodiment of all that was sweet, good, and true, in womanhood . . .

from *Illustrated Sydney News*, 1881

After all—

> The hand that rocks the cradle
> Is the hand that rules the world.

WILLIAM ROSS WALLACE, *John o'London's Treasure Trove*
[n.d.]

Source Acknowledgements

Ethel Berry, in Frances Backhouse (ed.), *Women of the Klondike* (Whitecap Books: Vancouver, 1995).

J. Boggie, *Experiences of Rhodesia's Pioneer Women* (Philpot & Collins: Bulawayo, 1938).

Lady Margaret Brooke, *Good Morning and Good Night* (Constable: London, 1934.

Jane Chadwick, *Memoirs*, Church Missionary Society Archive, University of Birmingham Library.

Louisa Clifton, *Diary* (MS 2801), printed by permission of the National Library of Australia.

Anna Cook, *Letters* (MS 849), printed by permission of the National Library of Australia.

Lady Denham, *United Empire Magazine*, 1930.

Ann Dundas, *Beneath African Glaciers* (H. F. & G. Witherby: London, 1924).

Alma E. M. Felt, *Memoirs*, printed by permission of Caroline Schimmel.

Ella Frances Fitz, *Lady Sourdough* (MacMillan: New York, 1951).

Mrs Flemming, in Patrick O'Farrell (ed.), *Letters from Irish Australia* (Belfast: Ulster Historical Foundation; Kensington, NSW: New South Wales University Press, 1984).

Eliza Flower, in Janet Walker and Richard Burkhardt, *Eliza Julia Flower: Letters of an English Gentlewoman: Life on the Illinois and Indiana Frontier 1817–1861* (Ball State University: Muncie, Indiana, 1991), reprinted by permission on Janet Walker and Richard W. Burkhardt.

M. Fountain and M. Spathaky (eds.), *Jessie's Sea Diary of 1861–62* (Cree Family History Society, 1994), reprinted by permission of Mr J. Cree Brown and the Cree Family History Society.

Charlotte Godley, *Letters from Early New Zealand* (Whitcombe and Tombs: Christchurch NZ, 1936).

J. Harcourt, *Diary*, printed by permission of the Maritime Archives and Library, Liverpool.

Isabella Hercus, *Journal*, printed by permission of the Maritime Archives and Library, Liverpool.

Madeleine Jackson, *Reminiscences*, British Library Department of Western Manuscripts.

H. H. Langton (ed.), *A Gentlewoman in Upper Canada* (Clarke, Irwin: Toronto, 1950).

Phoebe Langton, *Letter*, Alexander Turnbull Library, in F. Porter and C.

MacDonald (eds.), *My Hand will Write what my Heart Dictates* (Auckland University Press, 1996).

Margaret MacLeod (ed.), *Letters of Letitia Hargrave* (Champlain Society: Toronto, 1947), reprinted by permission of the Champlain Society.

Mrs Martineau, in Arnold Curtis (ed.), *Memories of Kenya* (Evans: London, 1986).

Mrs Moger, *Letter* (MS 5919), printed by permission of the National Library of Australia.

Lillian Moore, *Reminiscences*, printed by permission of Mrs Valerie Ruddock.

New Horizons: A Hundred Years of Women's Migration, printed by permission of the Archive of the Women's Migration Society, Fawcett Library.

Elise Pinckney, *The Letterbook of Eliza Pinckney* (University of North Carolina Press: Chapel Hill, 1972), reprinted by permission of The South Carolina Historical Society.

Eliza Lucas Pinckney, *Diary*, in Sandra Myres, *Westering Women* (University of New Mexico Press, 1982).

Rose Annie Rogers, *The Lonely Island* (G. Allen & Unwin: London, 1926).

Mollie Dorsey Sanford, *The Journal* (University of Nebraska Press, 1976).

Anne Isabelle Smith, *Diary*, printed by permission of the Maritime Archives and Library, Liverpool.

Society for the Overseas Settlement of British Women, *How it Helps*, 1931 (pamphlet in The Fawcett Library, London Guildhall University).

Ella Sykes, *A Home Help in Canada* (Smith, Elder: London, 1912).

Joan Thomas (ed.), *The Sea Journals of Annie Henning* (Halstead Press: Sydney, 1984).

Kyffin Thomas (ed.), *The Diary of Mary Thomas* (W. K. Thomas & Co: Adelaide, 1925).

Elizabeth Tierney, *Diary* (MS 4935), National Library of Australia.

H. Tremlett, *With the Tin Gods* (John Lane: London, 1915).

Mary Walker in P. Bartley and C. Loxton (eds.), *Plains Women* (Cambridge University Press: Cambridge, 1991), reprinted by permission of Cambridge University Press.

Rachel Watt, in Arnold Curtis (ed.), *Memories of Kenya* (Evans: London, 1986).

Eliza White, original document in Alexander Turnbull Library, in F. Porter and C. Macdonald (eds.), *My Hand will Write what my Heart Dictates* (Auckland University Press, 1996).

Any errors or omissions in the above list are entirely unintentional. If notified the publisher will be pleased to make any additions or amendments at the earliest opportunity.

Index of Authors

175